EX LIBRIS

VINTAGE **CLASSICS**

JOSÉ SARAMAGO

José Saramago is one of the most important international writers of the last hundred years. Born in Portugal in 1922, he was in his sixties when he came to prominence as a writer with the publication of *Baltasar & Blimunda*. A huge body of work followed, translated into almost fifty languages, and in 1998 he was awarded the Nobel Prize for Literature. Saramago died in June 2010.

Margaret Jull Costa has translated works by Eça de Quiroz, Fernando Pessoa and José Régio, as well as a number of leading Spanish authors. Her translation of José Saramago's *All the Names* won the Weidenfeld Translation Prize.

ALSO BY JOSÉ SARAMAGO

Fiction

Manual of Painting and Calligraphy
Baltasar & Blimunda
The Year of the Death of Ricardo Reis
The Gospel According to Jesus Christ
The History of the Siege of Lisbon
Blindness
All the Names
The Tale of the Unknown Island
The Stone Raft
The Cave
The Double
Seeing
Death at Intervals
Cain

Non-fiction

Journey to Portugal
Small Memories

JOSÉ SARAMAGO

The Elephant's Journey

TRANSLATED FROM THE PORTUGUESE BY
Margaret Jull Costa

VINTAGE

2 4 6 8 10 9 7 5 3 1

Vintage
20 Vauxhall Bridge Road,
London SW1V 2SA

Vintage Classics is part of the Penguin Random House group of companies
whose addresses can be found at global.penguinrandomhouse.com.

Penguin
Random House
UK

First published with the title *A Viagem do Elefante*
by Editorial Caminho, SA, Lisbon in 2008
First published in Great Britain by Harvill Secker in 2010
This edition reissued by Vintage in 2017

www.vintage-books.co.uk

A CIP catalogue record for this book is available from the British Library

ISBN 9781784871796

This publication was assisted by a grant from the
Diracção-Geral do Livro e das Bibliotecas / Portugal

Ministério da Cultura

Direcção-Geral
do Livro e das
Bibliotecas

Printed and bound by Clays Ltd, St Ives plc

Penguin Random House is committed to a sustainable future
for our business, our readers and our planet. This book is made
from Forest Stewardship Council® certified paper.

MIX
Paper from
responsible sources
FSC
www.fsc.org   FSC® C018179

If Gilda Lopes Encarnação had not been Portuguese *leitora* at the University of Salzburg, if I had not been invited to talk to her students there, and if Gilda had not arranged for us to have supper in a restaurant called 'The Elephant', this book would not exist. Certain unknown fates came together that night in the city of Mozart in order that this writer would ask: 'What are those carvings over there?' The carvings were small wooden sculptures lined up in a row, and the first of them was Lisbon's Torre de Belém. This was followed by representations of various European buildings and monuments that clearly marked an itinerary. I was told that they illustrated the journey from Lisbon to Vienna made by an elephant in the sixteenth century, in 1551 to be precise, when João III was on the throne of Portugal. I sensed that there could be a story in this and said as much to Gilda Lopes Encarnação. She thought so too and undertook to help me gather the necessary historical facts. This book is the result of that chance encounter and owes an enormous debt to my providential supper companion, to whom I wish to express my deepest gratitude, as well as my esteem and respect.

José Saramago

For Pilar, who wouldn't let me die

In the end, we always arrive at the place where we are expected.

Book of Itineraries

Strange though it may seem to anyone unaware of the importance of the marital bed in the efficient workings of public administration, regardless of whether that bed has been blessed by church or state or no one at all, the first step of an elephant's extraordinary journey to austria, which we propose to describe hereafter, took place in the royal apartments of the portuguese court, more or less at bedtime. And it is no mere accident that we chose to use the vague expression more or less. For this enables us, with admirable elegance, to avoid having to go into details of a physical and physiological nature, often sordid and almost always ridiculous, and which, set down on paper, would offend the strict catholicism of dom joão the third, king of portugal and of the algarves, and of dona catarina of austria, his wife and the future grandmother of the same dom sebastião who will go off to lead the attack on alcácer-quibir and die there during the first assault, or perhaps the second, although there are also those who say he died of an illness on the eve of battle. This is what the king, with furrowed brow, said to the queen, I'm worried about something, my lady, About what, my lord, The gift we gave to our cousin maximilian at the time of his marriage four years ago always seemed to me unworthy of his lineage and his merits, and now that we have him close to home, so to speak, in his role as regent of spain in the city of valladolid, I would like to offer him something more valuable, more striking, what do you think, my lady, A monstrance would be a good idea, my lord, a monstrance, I find, is always most welcome, perhaps because it has the virtue of combining material value and

1

spiritual significance, Our holy church would not appreciate such liberality, it doubtless still retains in its infallible memory cousin maximilian's confessed sympathies for the reforms of the lutheran protestants, or were they calvinists, I was never quite sure, Vade retro, satana, exclaimed the queen, crossing herself, such a thought had never even occurred to me, now I'll have to go to confession first thing in the morning, Why tomorrow in particular, my lady, given that it is your custom to go to confession every day, asked the king, Because of the vile idea that the enemy placed on my vocal cords, oh, I can feel my throat burning as if it had been scorched by a breath from hell itself. Accustomed to the queen's sensory excesses, the king shrugged and returned to the difficult task of finding a present that might satisfy archduke maximilian of austria. The queen was murmuring a prayer and had just begun another when, suddenly, she stopped and almost shouted out, There's always solomon, What, asked the king, perplexed by this untimely invocation of the king of judah, Yes, my lord, solomon the elephant, And what has the elephant got to do with anything, asked the king somewhat waspishly, He could be the gift, my lord, answered the queen, standing up, euphoric and very excited, He's not exactly an appropriate wedding present, That doesn't matter. The king nodded slowly three times, paused and then nodded another three times, after which he said, Yes, it's an interesting idea, It's more than interesting, it's a very good idea, an excellent idea, retorted the queen, unable to suppress a gesture of impatience, almost of insubordination, the creature came from india more than two years ago, and since then he's done nothing but eat and sleep, with his water trough always full and a constant supply of food, it's as if he were a kept beast, but one who'll never earn his keep, That's hardly the poor creature's fault, there's no suitable work for him here, unless we were to send him to the docks on the river tagus to transport planks, but the poor thing would only suffer, because his professional speciality is transporting felled trees, so much better suited to the curve of his trunk, Send him off to vienna, then, But how, asked the king, That's not our affair, once cousin maximilian is the owner, it will be a matter for him to resolve, he is, I assume, still in valladolid, As far as I know, yes, Obviously, solomon would have to travel to valladolid on foot, he has the legs for it after all, And then on to vienna as well, he'll have no alternative, It's a long way, said the queen, A very long way, agreed the king gravely, and added, I'll write to cousin maximilian tomorrow, and if he accepts, we'll have to agree dates and ascertain certain facts, for example, when he intends leaving for vienna, and how many days it would take for solomon to travel from lisbon to valladolid, after that, it's up to him, we wash our hands of the affair, Yes, we wash our hands, said the queen, but deep inside, which is where the contradictions of the self do battle, she felt a sudden sadness at the thought of sending solomon off to such distant lands and into the care of strangers.

Early the following morning, the king summoned his secretary, pêro de alcáçova carneiro, and dictated a letter that did not come out well at the first attempt, nor at the second or the third, and in the end it had to be handed over entirely to his secretary, who had the necessary rhetorical skills as well as a knowledge of the etiquette and epistolary formulae used between sovereigns, all of which he had learned at the best of all possible schools, namely, from his father, antónio carneiro, from whom he had inherited the post. The resulting letter was perfect as regards both penmanship and argument, not even omitting the theoretical possibility, diplomatically expressed, that the gift might not be to the liking of the archduke, who would, nevertheless, find it extremely hard to reply in the negative, for the king of portugal also stated, in a key passage in the letter, that there was nothing in the whole of his kingdom as precious as the elephant solomon, both because he represented the unifying force of the divine creation that connects and establishes a kinship between all the species, why, some even say that man himself was made out of what was left over after the elephant had been created, and because of the symbolic, intrinsic and worldly values that the creature embodied. When the letter had been signed and sealed, the king summoned his master of the horse, a gentleman who enjoyed his complete confidence and to whom he first summarised the contents of the missive, then ordered him to select an escort worthy of his rank, but one, above all, that would prove equal to the responsibility of the mission with which he was being charged. The gentleman kissed the hand of the king, who, with all the solemnity of an oracle, spoke these sibylline words, Be as swift as the north wind and as sure as the flight of the eagle, Yes, my lord. Then, the king adopted quite a different tone and offered some pieces of practical advice, I don't need to remind you to change horses as often as proves necessary, that is what staging-posts are for, and this is no time for false economies, I will give instructions for the stables to be supplied with more horses, and one other thing, I think you should, if you can, in order to gain time, try to sleep on your horse while you gallop along the roads of castile. The master of the horse did not understand the king's little joke, or else preferred to let it pass, and merely said, Your highness's

4

orders will be carried out to the letter, I pledge my word and my life on it, and then he withdrew, walking backwards and bowing every three steps. No one could have a finer master of the horse, said the king. The secretary decided not to give voice to the adulatory sentiment that would consist in saying that the king's master of the horse could hardly be anything else or behave any differently, given that he had been personally chosen by his royal highness. He had the feeling that he had said something similar only a few days before. At the time, he had recalled some advice of his father's, Be careful, my son, any flattering remark, if repeated too often, will always wear thin in the end and become, instead, as wounding as any insult. And so the secretary, although not for the same reasons as the master of the horse, also chose to say nothing. It was during this brief silence that the king finally gave expression to a worrying thought that had occurred to him on waking, I've been thinking, I feel that I should go and see solomon, Does your highness wish me to call the royal guard, asked the secretary, No, two pageboys will be more than enough, one to carry messages and the other to go and find out why the first has not yet returned, oh, and yourself, secretary, if you would care to accompany me, You do me great honour, highness, far more than I deserve, Perhaps I do so in order that you may deserve still more, like your father, may he rest in peace, Allow me to kiss your highness's hand with all the love and respect with which I kissed his, Now that is far more than I deserve, said the king, smiling, Ah, no one can outdo your highness in dialectic and response, Although there are those who say that the fates who presided over my birth did not endow me with a gift for words, Words are not everything, my lord, going to visit the

5

elephant solomon today is a poetic act and will perhaps be seen as such in the future, What is a poetic act, asked the king, No one knows, my lord, we only recognise it when it happens, So far, though, I have only mentioned my intention of visiting solomon, Ah, but the word of a king would, I'm sure, be enough, That, I believe, is what rhetoricians call irony, Forgive me, your highness, You are forgiven, secretary, and if all your sins are of like gravity, your place in heaven is guaranteed, Possibly, but I'm not sure that this would be the best time to go to heaven, What do you mean by that, There is the inquisition to consider, sir, confession and absolution are no longer the safe-conduct passes they once were, The inquisition will maintain unity among christians, that is its objective, And a very holy objective it is, highness, but what means will it use to achieve that, If the end is holy, then the means to that end will also be holy, retorted the king rather sharply, Forgive me, your highness, and may I, May you what, May I ask you to excuse me from today's visit to solomon, I feel that I would not prove to be very agreeable company for your highness, No, I will not excuse you, I need your presence in the enclosure, But why, sir, if I may be so bold as to ask, Because I lack the intelligence to know if what you termed a poetic act will take place or not, replied the king with a half-smile that gave his beard and moustache a mischievous, almost mephistophelian look, I await your orders, my lord, At five o'clock prompt, I want four horses to be brought round to the palace gate, and make sure that my mount is large, strong and docile, I've never been much of a rider and, I'm even less of one now, what with all the aches and pains that age brings with it, Yes, my lord, And choose the pageboys who are to come with me very carefully, I don't want the kind who laugh at the slightest thing, it makes me feel like wringing their necks, Yes, my lord.

In the end, they did not leave until half past five because the queen, when she found out about the planned excursion, declared that she wanted to go too. It was very hard to convince her that it made no sense at all to prepare a carriage merely to go as far as belém, where solomon's enclosure had been built. And you certainly don't intend going on horseback, said the king peremptorily, determined not to allow any arguments. The queen obeyed this ill-disguised prohibition and withdrew, muttering that no one in portugal, or indeed in the whole world, loved solomon as much as she did. As can be seen, the contradictions of the self were multiplying. Having called the poor animal a kept beast, the worst possible insult for an irrational creature who had been forced to labour in india, on no pay, for years and years, catarina of austria was now revealing a hint of chivalrous remorse that had almost led her to challenge, at least outwardly, the authority of her lord, her husband and her king. It was basically a storm in a teacup, a minor conjugal crisis that would, inevitably, vanish with the return of the master of the horse, regardless of what answer he might bring. If the archduke accepted the elephant, the problem would resolve itself or, rather, the journey to vienna would resolve it, and if he didn't accept it, then they would simply have to say, once again, with the centuries-old experience of all peoples, that, despite the disappointments, frustrations and disillusions that are the daily bread of men and elephants alike, life goes on. Solomon has no idea what awaits him. The master of the horse, the emissary of his fate, is riding towards valladolid, having recovered from the unfortunate results of trying to sleep while on horseback, and the king of portugal, with his modest escort of secretary and pageboys, is about to arrive at the river's edge at belém, within sight of the jerónimos monastery and solomon's enclosure. Given time, everything in the universe will dovetail perfectly with everything else. There is the elephant. Although he is smaller than his african relatives, one can still see, beneath the layer of dirt covering him, the fine figure nature had in mind when she created him. Why is the animal so dirty, asked the king, where is his keeper, I assume there is a keeper. A man with indian features approached, he was dressed in little more than rags, a mixture of his original clothes and others made locally, barely covered by or barely covering scraps of the more exotic fabrics that had arrived, along with the elephant, on that same body, two years before. He was the mahout. The secretary soon realised that the keeper had not recognised the king, and since this was clearly not the moment for any formal introductions, along the lines of, your highness, allow me to introduce solomon's keeper, and this, sir indian, is the king of portugal, dom joão the third, who will come to be known as dom joão the pious, instead, he ordered the two pageboys to go into the enclosure and inform the bewildered mahout of the titles and qualities of the bearded personage currently fixing him with a stern gaze that boded no good, It's the king. The man stopped, as if he had been struck by a bolt of lightning, and then made as if to escape, but the pageboys caught hold of him by his rags and propelled him towards the stockade. The king, meanwhile, was standing on a rustic ladder that had been propped against the stockade, and was observing the spectacle with an air of irritation and repugnance, regretting having given in to that early-morning impulse to pay a sentimental visit

8

to this pachyderm, to this ridiculous proboscidean more than four ells high, who, god willing, will soon be depositing his malodorous excretions on the pretentious austrian city of vienna. The blame, at least in part, lay with the secretary and his comment about poetic acts, a comment that was still going round and round in the king's head. He shot a challenging glance at the otherwise estimable functionary, who, as if he had read his mind, said, Your coming here, my lord, was, indeed, a poetic act, and the elephant was merely the pretext, nothing more. The king muttered some inaudible remark, then said in a clear, firm voice, I want that animal washed, right now. He felt like a king, he was a king, and that feeling is understandable when you consider that never in his entire life as monarch had he uttered such a sentence. The pageboys passed the sovereign's order on to the mahout, and the man ran to a shed in which were stored things that looked like and may well have been tools, as well as others that no one could have said quite what they were. Beside the shed was a building, presumably the keeper's house, made out of planks and with an unboarded roof. He returned carrying a long-handled broom, filled a bucket from the wine vat that served as water trough and set to work. The elephant's pleasure was plain to see. The water and the scrubbing motion of the broom must have awoken in him some pleasant memory, a river in india, the rough trunk of a tree, and the proof was that for as long as the washing lasted, a good half hour, he did not move from the spot, standing firm on his powerful legs, as if he were hypnotised. Knowing as one does the preeminent virtues of bodily cleanliness, it was no surprise to find that in the place where one elephant had been there now stood another. The dirt that had covered him before, and through which one could barely see his skin, had vanished beneath the combined actions of water and broom, and solomon revealed himself now in all his splendour. A somewhat relative splendour, it must be said. The skin of an asian elephant like solomon is thick, a greyish coffee colour and sprinkled with freckles and hairs, a permanent disappointment to the elephant, despite the advice he was always giving himself about accepting his fate and being contented with what he had and giving thanks to vishnu. He surrendered himself to being washed as if he were expecting a miracle, a baptism, but the result was there for all to see, hairs and freckles. The king had not visited the elephant for over a year, he had forgotten the details and did not like what he was seeing at all. Apart, that is, from the pachyderm's long tusks, resplendently white and only slightly curved, like two swords pointing forward. But there was worse. Suddenly, the king of portugal, and of the algarves, who, a little earlier, had been so thrilled to have found the perfect present to give the emperor charles the fifth's son-in-law, felt as if he were about to fall off the ladder and into the gaping maw of ignominy. This is what the king was thinking, What if the archduke doesn't like him, what if he finds him ugly, what if he accepts the gift in principle, sight unseen, then sends him back, how will I bear the shame of being slighted in the compassionate or ironic eyes of the european community. What do you think of him, what impression does the creature make on you, the king asked his secretary, desperate for the scrap of hope that could only come from him, Pretty and ugly, my lord, are merely relative terms, to the owl even his owlets are pretty, what I see here, to apply a general law to one particular case, is a magnificent example of the asian elephant, with all the hairs and freckles proper to its nature, which will be sure to delight the archduke and astonish not only the court and the population of vienna, but also the ordinary people who see him along the way. The king gave a sigh of relief, Yes, I suppose you're right, Indeed, sir, and if I know anything about that other nature, the human variety, I would even go so far as to say, if your majesty will allow me, that this elephant with its hairs and freckles will become a political tool of the first order for the archduke of austria, if he is as astute as the evidence thus far suggests. Help me down, this conversation is making me dizzy. With the help of the secretary and the two pageboys, the king managed, without too much difficulty, to descend the few rungs he had climbed. He took a deep breath when he felt terra firma beneath his feet again and, for no apparent reason, unless, and this is pure speculation, for it is far too early to know for sure, the sudden oxygenation of his blood and the consequent renewal of the blood circulating around his brain made him think of something which, in normal circumstances, would probably never have occurred to him. It was this, The man cannot possibly go to vienna looking like that, dressed in rags, so order two suits to be made for him, one for work, when he has to ride on top of the elephant, and the other for social occasions, so that he does not cut a poor figure at the austrian court, nothing fancy, you understand, but worthy of the country sending him there, Of course, my lord, By the way, what is his name. A page was despatched to find out, and the answer, passed on by the secretary, was more or less this, subhro. Subro, repeated the king, what kind of name is that, It's spelt with an h, sir, at least so he said, explained the secretary, We should have just called him joaquim when he first arrived in portugal, grumbled the king.

11

Three days later, towards the close of the afternoon, the master of the horse, at the head of his escort, its pomp now somewhat dimmed by the grime of the roads and the inevitable stench of sweat exuded by both equines and humans, dismounted at the palace gates, brushed off the dust, went up the steps and was hurriedly ushered into the antechamber by the lackey-in-chief, a title which, as we had best confess at once, may not actually have existed at the time, but seemed to us appropriate, given the fellow's own corporeal odour, which he positively oozed, a mixture of presumption and false humility. Anxious to know the archduke's answer, the king received the new arrival at once. The queen was also present in the state room, which, given the importance of the moment, should surprise no one, especially given that, at the behest of the king, she regularly participates in meetings of state, where she has always been more than a mere passive spectator. There was another reason why she wanted to hear the letter read out as soon as it arrived, for the queen nurtured the vague hope, however unlikely she knew this to be, that archduke maximilian's missive would be written in german, in which case she, the most highly placed of translators, would be there, on hand so to speak, ready to be of service. Meanwhile, the king had received the scroll from his master of the horse, and had himself unrolled it, once he had untied the ribbons sealed with the archduke's coat of arms, but a quick glance was enough for him to see that it was written in latin. Now dom joão, the third king of portugal to bear that name, although not entirely ignorant of the latin language, for he had studied

12

it in his youth, knew all too well that his inevitable stumb-
lings, prolonged pauses and downright errors of interpret-
ation would give those present a wretched and erroneous
impression of his royal self. The secretary, with the agility
of mind we have noted before and equally quick reflexes,
had already taken two discreet steps forward and was waiting.
In the most natural of tones, as if the scene had been
rehearsed, the king said, My secretary will read the letter,
translating into portuguese the message in which our beloved
cousin maximilian is doubtless responding to our offer of
the elephant solomon, it seems to me unnecessary to read
the whole letter now, all we need, at the moment, is the gist,
Of course, sir. The secretary ran his eyes over the super-
abundance of polite salutations, which, in the epistolary style
of the time, proliferated like mushrooms after rain, then
read further on and found what he was looking for. He did
not translate, he merely announced, The archduke maximilian of austria gratefully accepts the king of portugal's gift.
Among the hairy mass formed by beard and moustache, a
smile of satisfaction appeared on the royal face. The queen
smiled too, at the same time putting her hands together in
a gesture of gratitude which, while intended, first, for the
archduke maximilian of austria, had, as its ultimate recipi-
ent, almighty god. The contradictory feelings doing battle
inside the queen had reached a synthesis, the most banal of
all, namely that no one can escape his fate. The secretary
went on, explaining the further contents of the letter in a
voice in which the monastic gravity of the latin seemed to
find an echo in the day-to-day portuguese into which he
was translating. He says that he has not yet decided when
he will leave for vienna, possibly around the middle of
october, but he is not sure, And it's the beginning of August

already, said the queen rather unnecessarily, The archduke also says, sir, that if it suits your highness, you need not wait until a time nearer the date of his departure to send suleiman to valladolid, What suleiman is that, asked the king angrily, he hasn't even got the elephant yet and already he wants to change his name, Suleiman the magnificent, sir, the ottoman sultan, What would I do without you, secretary, how else could I possibly know who suleiman was if your brilliant memory were not there to enlighten and guide me at all times, Forgive me, sir, said the secretary. There was an awkward silence during which those present avoided looking at each other. The secretary's face, which had initially flushed bright red, was now deathly pale. No, I'm the one who should ask your forgiveness, said the king, and I do so unprompted save by the promptings of my own conscience, Sir, stammered pêro de alcáçova carneiro, who am I to forgive you anything, You're my secretary, to whom I have been disrespectful, Please, sir. The king made a gesture imposing silence, and then said, Solomon, as he will continue to be called for as long as he remains here, can have no idea of the anxiety he's caused us ever since the day I decided to make a present of him to the archduke, my feeling is that, deep down, no one here really wants him to go, it's odd, isn't it, he's not a cat who comes rubbing around our legs or a dog who gazes up at us as if we were its creator, and yet here we all are, in a state of distress and near despair, as if something were being wrenched from us, No one could have put it better, sir, said the secretary, But let us return to the matter in hand, now where had we got to in this business of despatching solomon to valladolid, asked the king, The archduke writes that it would be best if the elephant came sooner rather than later so that he can become accustomed to the change of

14

people and surroundings, well, the latin word he uses doesn't mean quite that, but it's the best I can find at the moment, Well, don't go racking your brains any further, we understand what you mean, said the king. Then, after a moment's reflection, he added, My master of the horse will be in charge of organising the expedition, he'll need two men to help the mahout in his work, plus a few more to ensure that there are always plentiful supplies of food and water, an ox-cart just in case one proves necessary, for example, to transport the elephant's water trough, although in portugal, of course, there'll be no shortage of rivers or riverbanks where solomon can drink and wallow, although they might meet problems in that wretched place castile, which is always as dry as a bone left out in the sun, and, finally, a troop of cavalry in the unlikely event of someone trying to steal our precious solomon, our master of the horse will give our secretary of state regular progress reports, and forgive me, secretary, for involving you in such trivialities, Hardly trivialities, sir, the matter is of particular relevance to me since what we're dealing with here is neither more nor less than the transfer of a state asset, Solomon, I'm sure, has never thought of himself as a state asset, said the king with a wry smile, He would only have to consider, sir, that the water he drinks and the food he eats do not fall from the heavens, Well, as far as I'm concerned, said the queen, I hereby give orders that no one should come and tell me when solomon has left, I will ask when I'm ready to know and only then will I expect an answer. This last word was barely audible, as if tears had suddenly constricted the royal throat. A queen crying is a spectacle from which, out of decency, we are all obliged to avert our gaze. Which is precisely what the king, the secretary of state and the master of the horse did. Then, once she had left and the rustle of her skirts on the floor had ceased to be heard, the king said, You see, that's what I mean, none of us wants solomon to go, It's not too late for a change of heart, sir, Oh, my heart has changed, no doubt about that, but time has run out, solomon is already on his way, Your highness has more important matters to deal with, don't allow an elephant to become the centre of your concerns, What's the mahout's name, the king asked suddenly, Subhro, I believe, sir, What does it mean, I don't know, sir, but I could ask him, Yes, do, I want to know into whose hands I am entrusting solomon, The same hands he was in before, sir, for, if I may make so bold as to remind you, the elephant travelled from india with the very same mahout, Being far away and being near at hand changes everything, up until now, I never cared what the man's name was, but now I do, Of course, sir, I understand, That's what I like about you, secretary, you don't need to have things spelled out in order to understand what a person means, My father was a good teacher and your highness is in no way his inferior, Such praise is, at first glance, of little worth, but since you're measuring me against your father, it pleases me, May I withdraw, sir, asked the secretary, Yes, go about your business, and don't forget those new clothes for the mahout, what did you say his name was again, Subhro, sir, with an h, Right.

Ten days after this conversation, when the sun had barely appeared above the horizon, solomon finally left the enclosure in which he had languished for two years. The convoy was precisely as the king had ordered, with the mahout, who presided from on high, seated on the elephant's back, the two men who were there to help him in whatever way proved necessary, the other men in charge of food supplies, the ox-cart bearing the water trough, which the bumps in the road constantly sent sliding from one side to the other, as well as a gigantic load of fodder of varying types, the cavalry troop who were responsible for security along the way and the safe arrival of all concerned, and, finally, something that the king had not thought of, the quarter-master's wagon drawn by two mules. The absence of curious onlookers and other witnesses could be explained by the extremely early hour and the secrecy that had shrouded the departure, although there was one exception, a royal carriage that set off in the direction of Lisbon as soon as elephant and company had disappeared around the first bend in the road. Inside were the king of portugal, dom joão the third, and his secretary of state, pêro de alcáçova carneiro, whom we may not see again, although perhaps we will, because life laughs at predictions and introduces words where we imagined silences, and sudden returns when we thought we would never see each other again. I've forgotten the meaning of the mahout's name, what was it again, the king was asking, White, sir, subhro means white, although you'd never think it to look at him. In a room in the palace, in the gloom of the bed canopy, the sleeping queen is having a nightmare. She

17

is dreaming that solomon has been taken from belém and that she keeps asking everyone, Why didn't you tell me, but when she does finally decide to wake up, around midmorning, she will not repeat that question and cannot be sure that she, on her own initiative, ever will. It may be that in the next few years, someone will chance to mention the word elephant in her presence and then the queen of portugal, catherine of austria, will say, Speaking of elephants, whatever happened to solomon, is he still in belém or has he already been dispatched to vienna, and when they tell her that he is indeed in vienna, living in a kind of zoological garden along with other wild animals, she will respond, feigning innocence, What a fortunate creature, there he is enjoying life in the most beautiful city in the world, and here am I, trapped between today and the future and with no hope in either of them. The king, if he's present, will pretend not to hear, and the secretary of state, the same pêro de alcáçova carneiro whom we have already met, even though he is not a man given to praying, we need only recall what he said about the inquisition and, more importantly, what he thought best not to say, will offer up a silent prayer to heaven asking for the elephant to be enveloped in a thick cloak of oblivion that will so disguise his shape that he could be mistaken by lazy imaginations for that other strange-looking beast, the dromedary, or for some other type of camel, whose unfortunate two-humped appearance would be unlikely to linger in the memory of anyone interested in these insignificant events. The past is an immense area of stony ground that many people would like to drive across as if it were a motorway, while others move patiently from stone to stone, lifting each one because they need to know what lies beneath. Sometimes scorpions crawl out or centipedes, fat white caterpillars or ripe chrysalises, but it's not impossible that, at least once, an elephant might appear, and that the elephant might carry on its shoulders a mahout named subhro, meaning white, an entirely inappropriate word to describe the man who, in the sight of the king of portugal and his secretary of state, appeared in the enclosure in belém, looking every bit as filthy as the elephant he was supposed to be taking care of. There may be some truth in the wise saying that warns us that even the brightest blade grows dim with rust, because that is precisely what had happened to the mahout and his elephant. When they first fetched up in belém, popular curiosity reached astonishing heights and the court itself organised select excursions comprising noblemen and noblewomen, ladies and gentlemen, to view the pachyderm, however, that initial interest soon faded, and the result was plain to see, the mahout's indian clothes were transformed into rags and the elephant's hairs and freckles had almost vanished beneath the crust of dirt accumulated over two years. This is not the case now, however. Although the inevitable dust from the road is already coating his legs from foot to knee, solomon nevertheless walks proudly along, as clean as a new pin, and the mahout, although no longer dressed in colourful indian garb, is resplendent in his new uniform for which, even better, either out of forgetfulness or generosity on the part of his employers, he had not had to pay. Sitting astride the part of the elephant where neck meets sturdy body and wielding the stick with which he steers his mount, one moment delivering light flicks, the next sharp jabbing movements that leave their mark on the animal's tough skin, the mahout subhro, or white, is about to become the second or third most important character in the story, the first being the elephant solomon, who, naturally, takes precedence as the main protagonist, followed by the aforementioned subhro and the archduke, jockeying with each other for the lead role, now this one, now that. However, the character currently occupying centre stage is the mahout. Glancing from one end of the convoy to the other, he cannot help but notice its distinctly motley appearance, understandable given the diversity of animals involved, namely, elephant, men, horses, mules and oxen, each walking at a different pace, either natural or enforced, because on a journey such as this no one can go much faster than the slowest, and the slowest, of course, are the oxen. The oxen, said subhro, suddenly alarmed, where are the oxen. Not a sign of them, nor of the heavy load they were pulling, the trough full of water and the bundles of forage. They must have got left behind, he thought, reassuring himself, there's nothing for it but to wait. He prepared to slide down from the elephant's back, but stopped. He might have to get back on again and not be able to. In principle, the elephant would proffer his trunk to raise him up and practically deposit him on his seat. However, prudence told him that one should always foresee situations in which the animal, out of ill-will, irritation or sheer contrariness, might refuse to offer his services as a lift, which is where the ladder came in, although it was hard to believe that an angry elephant would agree to be a mere support and unresistingly allow the mahout or whoever to climb aboard. The ladder was of merely symbolic value, like a small reliquary worn round the neck or a medal bearing the figure of some saint. In this case, though, he could not make use of the ladder because it was on the cart that had fallen behind. Subhro summoned one of his assistants so that he could warn the commanding officer of the cavalry troop that they would have to wait for the ox-cart. Besides, the rest would do the horses good, although, if truth be told, they had hardly had to exert themselves, never once breaking into a gallop or even a trot, but proceeding at a sedate walking pace. This was nothing like the master of the horse's recent expedition to valladolid, which was still fresh in the memories of those who had gone with him, veterans of that heroic cavalcade. The horsemen dismounted, the men on foot sat or lay down on the ground, and several took the opportunity to have a nap. From his perch high up on the elephant, the mahout reviewed the journey so far and was not pleased. To judge by the height of the sun, they must have been walking for about three hours, although that put rather too favourable a gloss on things because some considerable part of that time had been taken up with solomon's long bathing sessions in the river tagus, which alternated with voluptuous wallowings in the mud, which, in turn, according to elephant logic, called for further prolonged baths. It was clear that solomon was excited and nervous, and needed to be treated with great patience and calm. We must have wasted a good hour on solomon's little games, thought the mahout, and then, passing from a reflection on time to a meditation on space, How far have we travelled, a league, possibly two, he wondered. A cruel doubt, an urgent question. If we were still living among the ancient greeks and romans, we would say, with the serenity that practical knowledge always confers, that the main itinerary measures of distance at the time were the stadium, the mile and the league. Setting aside the stadium and the mile, with their divisions into feet and paces, let us consider the league, which was the word used by subhro, a distance that was also composed of paces and feet, but which has the enormous advantage of placing us in familiar territory. Yes, but everyone knows what leagues are, our contemporaries will say with an ironic smile. The best answer we can give them is this, Yes, everyone did in the age in which they lived, but only in the age in which they lived. The old word league, or leuga, which should, one would think, have meant the same to everyone at all times, has in fact made a long journey from the seven thousand five hundred feet or one thousand five hundred paces of the romans and the early middle ages to the kilometres and metres with which we now divide up distance, no less than five and five thousand respectively. It's the same with other measurements as well. And if you need evidence to back this statement up, consider the case of the almude, a measure of capacity that was divided into twelve canadas or forty-eight quarts, and which, in lisbon, was equal, in round numbers, to sixteen and a half litres, and in oporto, to twenty-five litres. How did they manage, the curious reader and lover of learning will ask, How do *we* manage, asks the person who first mentioned this whole weights and meas-ures problem, thus skilfully avoiding giving an answer. Now, having presented the matter with such dazzling clarity, we can make an absolutely crucial, almost revolutionary decision, namely this, while the mahout and his companions, given that they would have no other means at their disposal, will continue to speak of distances in accord with the uses and customs of their age, we, so that we can understand what is going on in this regard, will use our own modern itinerary units of measurement, which will avoid constantly having to resort to tiresome conversion tables. It will be as if we were adding subtitles in our own language to a film, a concept unknown in the sixteenth century, to compensate for our ignorance or imperfect knowledge of the language spoken by the actors. We will, therefore, have two parallel discourses that will never meet, this one, which we will be able to follow without difficulty and another, which, from this moment on, will remain silent. An interesting solution.

All these observations, ponderings and cogitations led the mahout finally to descend from the elephant's back via its trunk and to stride boldly over to the cavalry troop. It was easy enough to find the commanding officer. There was a kind of awning that was doubtless protecting some eminent personage from the punishing august sun, so the conclusion was easy to draw, if there was an awning, there must be a commanding officer beneath it, and if there was a commanding officer, there would have to be an awning to protect him. The mahout had an idea which he didn't quite know how to introduce into the conversation, but the commanding officer unwittingly made his job easy, Where have those oxen got to, he asked, Well, I haven't actually seen them yet, sir, but they should be here any moment, Let's hope so. The mahout took a deep breath and said in a voice hoarse with excitement, If you'll permit me, sir, I've had an idea, If you've already had the idea, you obviously don't need my permission, You're quite right, sir, forgive my imperfect grasp of grammar, Tell me what your idea is then, The main problem is the oxen, Yes, they haven't yet arrived, What I mean, sir, is that the problem will remain the same even once they have arrived, Why, Because oxen are, by nature, very slow creatures, sir, Well, that much I know, and I don't need an indian to tell me, If we had another pair of oxen and yoked them up to the cart we already have, we would be able to travel more quickly and all at the same pace, Sounds like a good idea, but where are we going to find another pair of oxen, There are villages nearby, sir. The commanding officer frowned, he could not deny that there were indeed villages nearby where they could buy a pair of oxen. Although why buy them, he thought, we'll requisition the oxen in the name of the king and, on the way back from valladolid, leave them here, in as good a state as I hope they'll be in now. Just then, a roar went up, the oxen had finally come into view, the men applauded and even the elephant raised his trunk and trumpeted contentedly. His poor sight did not allow him to see the bundles of forage from that distance, but the vast cavern of his stomach echoed with protests that it was high time he had something to eat. This doesn't mean that a healthy elephant has to eat at regular hours like a human being. Amazing though it may seem, an elephant gets through about two hundred litres of water a day and between one hundred and fifty and three hundred kilos of forage. So we shouldn't imagine him with a napkin tied around his neck and sitting down at table to eat his three square meals a day, no, an elephant eats what he can, as much as he can and where he can, and his guiding principle is not to leave anything behind that he might need later on. He still had to wait nearly half an hour before the ox-cart arrived. Meanwhile, the commanding officer gave the order to pitch camp, although they first had to find a place less exposed to the sun if soldiers and civilians were not to be burnt to a crisp. About five hundred metres away there was a small copse of poplar trees for which the company duly headed. The shade was fairly sparse, but better that than stay and roast beneath the implacable metal disc of the king of planets. The men who had come with the party in order to work and of whom very little, indeed absolutely nothing, had so far been required, had the usual kind of food in their saddlebags and haversacks, a large piece of bread, some dried sardines, a few dried figs, and a wedge of goat's cheese, of the sort that becomes hard as stone and which, rather than chew, you have to gnaw at patiently, thus allowing you to enjoy the flavour for longer. As for the soldiers, they had their own arrangements. A cavalryman, with sword unsheathed or spear at the ready, whether charging the enemy at a gallop or simply accompanying an elephant to valladolid, has no need to worry about supplies. He's not interested in where the food comes from or who prepares it, what matters is that his plate is full and the stew not entirely inedible. In scattered groups, everyone, apart from solomon, was now busily engaged in masticatory and deglutitory activities. Subhro, the mahout, gave the order for two bundles of forage to be carried to where solomon was waiting his turn, to untie them and leave him be, If necessary, take him another bundle, he said. Many will doubtless disapprove of this deliberate excess of detail, but this description serves a useful purpose, that of encouraging subhro's mind to reach an optimistic conclusion regarding the future of this journey, If solomon eats at least three or four bundles of forage a day, he thought, the weight in the cart will gradually be reduced and if we get that extra pair of oxen, then, however many mountains may step into our path, there'll be no holding us. The same thing happens with good ideas, and, on occasions, with bad ones, as happens with democritus' atoms or with cherries in a basket, they come along linked one to the other. When subhro imagined the oxen pulling the cart up a steep hill, he realised that a mistake had been made in the original composition of the convoy, a mistake that had not been corrected during the journey so far, an oversight for which he considered himself responsible. The thirty men who had come as assistants, and whom subhro took the trouble to count one by one, had done nothing since their departure from lisbon, apart from going off for morning walks in the countryside. The two men on the ox-cart would be perfectly capable of untying and dragging the bundles of forage over to solomon, and in case of need, he himself could always lend a hand. What should I do, send them back, and free myself of that weight of responsibility, wondered subhro. That would have been a good idea if there hadn't been a better one. The idea brought a bright smile to the mahout's face. He shouted to the men and gathered them round him, some of them still chewing on their last dried fig, and he said, From now on, you will be divided into two groups, in order to help push or pull the ox-cart, because the load is clearly too much for the animals, who are, besides, slow by nature, so, every two kilometres, the groups will swap over, and that will be your principal work until we reach valladolid. There was a murmur of what sounded very much like discontent, but subhro pretended not to hear it and went on, Each group will have a foreman, who, as well as having to answer to me for the good results of the work, will have to maintain discipline and develop the team spirit essential in any collective task. This language obviously failed to please his audience, because the same murmur was repeated. Fine, said subhro, if anyone is unhappy with the orders I've just given, he can go to the commanding officer, who, as the king's representative, is the supreme authority here. The air seemed suddenly to grow colder, and the murmur was replaced by an embarrassed scuffling of feet. Subhro asked, Right, any volunteers for the post of foreman. Three hesitant hands went up, and the mahout explained, I need two foremen, not three. One of the hands shrank back, disappeared, while the others remained raised. You and you, said subhro, choose your men, but do so in an equitable manner, so that the strength of the two groups is evenly balanced, and now off you go, I need to speak to the commanding officer. Before he did so, however, he was obliged to attend to one of his assistants, who had approached to inform him that they had untied another bundle of forage, but that solomon appeared to have had enough and all the signs were that he wanted to sleep, I'm not surprised, he's eaten well and this is the time he usually takes his nap, The trouble is he's drunk nearly all the water in the trough, Well, that's only natural after eating so much, We could take the oxen down to the river, there must be a path somewhere, He wouldn't drink the water from that part of the river, it's still salty, How do you know, asked one assistant, Because solomon has bathed in the river several times, the last time just near here, and he never once put his trunk in to drink, If the sea water comes up as far as this, that only shows what a short distance we've covered, True enough, but I can assure you that we'll be travelling much faster from now on, my word as a mahout. Leaving behind him this solemn commitment, subhro went in search of the commanding officer. He found him asleep in the shade of one of the more densely leaved poplars, sleeping the light sleep that marks out the good soldier, always ready to pick up his weapons at the slightest suspicious noise. He was guarded by two soldiers who, with an authoritative gesture, ordered subhro to stop. Subhro raised his hand to indicate that he had understood and sat down on the ground to wait. The commanding officer woke up half an hour later, stretched and yawned, then yawned and stretched again, until he felt that he had properly reawoken to life. Nevertheless, he had to look twice when he saw that the mahout was there again, What do you want now, he asked gruffly, don't tell me you've had another idea, Indeed I have, sir, Out with it then, Well, I've divided the men into two groups and they're going to take turns, every two or so kilometres, in helping the oxen, that will mean fifteen men at a time pushing the cart, you'll definitely notice the difference, Good thinking, no doubt about it, that round thing on your shoulders obviously serves some purpose, and my horses will certainly feel the benefit, being able to break into a trot now and then, rather than trudging along at parade-ground pace, Yes, that occurred to me too, sir, And to judge by the look on your face, something else has occurred to you as well, hasn't it, asked the commanding officer, Yes, sir, it has, What is it then, It seems to me that we should organise our lives in accord-ance with solomon's needs and habits, right now, for example, he's asleep, and if we woke him up, he'd be really irritable and only cause us trouble, But how can he possibly sleep standing up, asked the commanding officer, incredulous, He does lie down to sleep sometimes, but normally he sleeps on his feet, Hm, I really don't think I'll ever understand elephants, Well, I've been working with them almost since I was born and I still can't understand them, And why is that, Perhaps because an elephant is much more than just an elephant, Right, that's enough talk, But I have another idea to put to you, sir, Another idea, said the officer, laughing, you're clearly no ordinary mahout, you're a veritable mine of ideas, You're too kind, sir, What else has that remarkable mind of yours produced, Well, I thought that since it's the cart that's setting the pace, it might be a better plan if you brought up the rear with your soldiers, with the ox-cart at the front, followed by me and the elephant, the men on foot and the quartermaster's wagon, Now that's what I call an idea, Yes, I thought so too, A stupid idea, I mean, Why, asked subhro, stung, and unaware of the insulting nature of that blunt question asked directly of an officer, Because I and my soldiers would have to eat the dust kicked up by the feet of everyone else in front, Oh, how dreadful, I should have thought of that and I didn't, I beg you, sir, by all the saints in heaven's court, to forgive me, So what we'll do is gallop ahead now and then and wait for the rest of you to catch up, Yes, sir, that seems the perfect solution, may I go now, asked subhro, Wait, I have two further matters to take up with you, the first is this, if you ever again ask me why in the tone of voice you did just now, I will give orders for you to receive a good ration of lashes on your back, Yes, sir, murmured subhro, head bowed, The second has to do with that head on your shoulders and with this journey that has barely begun, I would like to know, always assuming there are still any useful ideas left in that noddle of yours, if you expect us to stay here until the end of time, for ever and ever, amen, Solomon is still asleep, sir, So the elephant's in charge here, is he, asked the commanding officer, half-annoyed and half-amused, No, sir, but you will doubtless recall that I mentioned earlier organising ourselves in accordance with, and I confess I don't know where I got that expression from, solomon's needs and habits, Meaning what, asked the commanding officer, who was beginning to lose patience, Well, solomon, in order to be at his best, and so that we can deliver him in good health to the archduke of austria, needs to rest during the hottest part of the day, Agreed, replied the commanding officer, slightly troubled by this reference to the archduke, but the fact is he has done almost nothing but sleep all day, Today doesn't count, sir, it's the first day and, as everyone knows, nothing ever goes well on the first day, So what should we do, We divide the days into three parts, the first, from early morning on, the third, lasting

29

until sunset, so that we advance as quickly as we can, the second part of the day, where we are now, should be set aside for eating and resting, That seems to me a good plan, said the commanding officer, deciding to opt for a more benevolent attitude. The change of tone encouraged the mahout to express the troubling thought that had been bothering him all day, There's something about this journey, sir, that I don't understand, And what is that, We haven't met a soul all the time we've been travelling and that, in my modest opinion, does not seem normal, You're mistaken, we've met quite a lot of people, coming from both directions, How is it I didn't see them then, asked subhro, his eyes wide with surprise, You were bathing the elephant, Do you mean to say that people passed each time solomon was taking a bath, Don't make me repeat myself, That's a strange coincidence, it's almost as if solomon didn't want to be seen, That's possible, yes, But we've been camped here for a good few hours now and no one has passed, That's for a different reason, people see the elephant in the distance, like a ghost, and immediately turn back or take a different route, perhaps thinking that solomon has been sent by the devil, How extraordinary, why, it had even occurred to me that our king had given orders to clear the roads, You're not that important, No, I'm not, but solomon is. The officer preferred not to respond to what seemed to be the beginning of a whole new discussion and said, Before you go, I'd like to ask you something, Please, I'm all ears, Do you remember, just now, having invoked all the saints in heaven's court, Yes, sir, I do, Does that mean you're a christian, now think carefully before you answer, More or less, sir, more or less.

A full moon, august moonlight. Everyone is sleeping, with the exception of the two mounted guards patrolling the camp, the only sound the creaking of leather. The sleepers are enjoying a well-deserved rest, for although, during the first part of the day, the men enlisted to push the ox-cart may have given the impression of being a band of lazy good-for-nothings, they had set to work with great brio and shown themselves to be out-and-out professionals. True, the flat terrain had helped a great deal, but you could safely bet that, in the whole venerable history of that ox-cart, there had never been a day like it. During the three and a half hours they had been travelling, and despite a few short breaks, they had covered more than seventeen kilometres. This was the figure finally decided upon by the commanding officer after a lively exchange of words with the mahout subhro, who thought that the distance had been somewhat shorter and that it was best not to deceive themselves. The commanding officer disagreed, believing that it would help to encourage the men, What difference does it make if we did only travel fourteen kilometres, we'll cover the missing three tomorrow and it'll all work out in the end, you'll see. The mahout gave up trying to persuade him, I did my best, he thought, and if the commanding officer's false accounting prevailed, that doesn't alter the reality of the kilometres we really did travel, yes, subhro, you really must learn not to argue with the man in charge.

He had woken with the impression that he had experienced a sharp pain in his stomach while sleeping, and although it seemed to him unlikely that this would recur,

31

his insides felt suspiciously restless, with a few silent gurglings in his intestines, and then suddenly there it was again, that same stabbing pain. He got up as quickly as he could, indicated to the nearest guard that he needed to leave the encampment and then strode towards a dense row of trees at the top of the gentle slope on which they had pitched camp, so gentle that it was as if they were lying in a bed with the bedhead slightly raised. He arrived just in time. Let us avert our gaze while he takes down his breeches, which, miraculously, he has not yet soiled, and wait for him to look up and see what we have seen already, a village bathed in the marvellous august moonlight that moulded every contour, softened the very shadows it created and, at the same time, illuminated the places where it fell unimpeded. The words we were waiting for finally appeared, A village, a village. Doubtless because they were tired, no one else had yet thought to climb the hill to see what was on the other side. It's always good to see a village, if not this one then another, but it seems improbable that in the very first one we come across we'll find a powerful pair of oxen capable of righting the leaning tower of pisa with a single tug. Having finished his urgent business, the mahout cleaned himself as best he could with a handful of the greenery growing round about, and it was fortunate indeed that no nettles, also known as fire-weed, were to be found, because they would have made him leap about like a victim of saint vitus dance, so badly would they have burnt and stung his delicate lower mucous membrane. A thick cloud suddenly covered the moon, and the village was plunged in darkness, as if it had vanished like a dream into the surrounding gloom. It didn't matter, the sun would rise at the appropriate hour and show the way to the stable, where the ruminating oxen already had a sixth sense that their lives were about to change. Subhro walked back through the dense trees and returned to his place alongside the other men in the encampment. On the way, it occurred to him that if the commanding officer was awake, this information would give him the greatest satisfaction in the world, to resort to grandiose planetary terminology. And the glory of having discovered the village would be all mine, he murmured. Because there was no point in fostering vain illusions. During what remained of the night, other men might feel the need to empty their bowels, and the only place where they could do so discreetly was in the middle of those trees, but even supposing that this didn't happen, it would only be a matter of waiting for the dawn when we would witness a whole procession of men obeying the calls of intestines and bladder, hardly surprising given that we're all animals under the skin. Feeling mildly disgruntled, the mahout decided to make a detour to the place where the commanding officer was sleeping, you never know, sometimes people suffer from insomnia or wake up distraught because they had a dream that they were dead, or else were being bitten by a bedbug, one of the many that hide in the hems of blankets, come to drink the sleeper's blood. Let it be set down here, by the way, that the bedbug was the unwitting inventor of blood transfusions. Vain hope. The commanding officer was sleeping, and not just sleeping, but snoring. A guard came over to ask the mahout what he was doing there, and subhro replied that he had a message for the commanding officer, but seeing that he was asleep, he would return to his own bed, This is no time to be giving anyone messages, wait until morning, It's important, answered the mahout, but, as elephant philosophy would have it, what cannot be cannot be, If you'd like to give me

33

the message, I'll pass it on to him as soon as he wakes up. The mahout considered the favourable probabilities and decided that it was worth betting on this one card, that the guard would already have informed the commanding officer of the village's existence when, at first light, the cry went up, Village ahoy. Hard experience of life has shown us that, generally speaking, it is inadvisable to trust too much in human nature. From now on, we will also know that we should not trust the cavalry either, at least when it comes to keeping secrets. Thus, even before the mahout had fallen asleep again, the other guard had already learned the news, and shortly after that, all the soldiers sleeping nearby knew as well. There was intense excitement, with one soldier even suggesting a reconnaissance trip to the village in order to collect first-hand information, which, given the authenticity of the source, would help strengthen the strategy to be drawn up in the morning. Fear that the commanding officer might wake, get out of bed and find none of the soldiers there, or worse still, find some and not others, forced them to abandon this promising adventure. The hours passed, a pale glow in the east began to trace the curved outline of the door through which the sun would enter, while, on the opposite side, the moon was slipping gently into the arms of another night. And we were thus engaged, postponing the moment of revelation, still wondering if there wasn't perhaps another more dramatic solution to be found, or, which would be the icing on the cake, one with more symbolic power, when the fateful cry rang out, There's a village over there. Absorbed in our own lucubrations, we had failed to notice that a man had got up and climbed the slope, but now we see him appear among the trees, we hear him repeat the triumphal news, although the words he uses are not, as we had imagined,

34

Village ahoy, but There's a village over there. It was the commanding officer. Destiny, when it chooses, is as good or even better than god at writing straight on crooked lines. Sitting on his blanket, subhro thought, It could be worse, he could always say that he had got up in the middle of the night and been the first to see the village. He'll risk the commanding officer asking him scornfully, as we know he will, And do you have witnesses, to which he will have to reply, metaphorically putting his tail between his legs, No, sir, I was alone, You must have dreamed it then, Not only did I not dream it, I gave the information to one of your guards so that he would tell you when you woke up, None of my soldiers spoke to me about this, But you could speak to him, I'll tell you which one it was. The commanding officer reacted badly to this proposal, If I didn't need you to ride the elephant, I would send you straight back to lisbon, and imagine your position then, it would be your word against mine, and I leave you to draw your own conclusions as to the result, or do you want to be deported to india. Having resolved the question of who, officially, had been the first to discover the village, the commanding officer was about to turn his back on the mahout when the latter said, That isn't what matters, what matters is finding out if the village has a decent pair of oxen, We'll find out soon enough, meanwhile, you take care of your business and leave the rest to me, Don't you want me to go to the village, sir, asked subhro, No, I don't, I'll take the sergeant with me and the ox-driver. For once, Subhro agreed with the commanding officer. If anyone had a natural right to be there it was the ox-driver. The commanding officer was already busily issuing orders to the sergeant and to the quartermaster's men, whom he now wanted to provide food both for the soldiers and for the strong men pushing or pulling the cart, for they would lose what strength they had in no time if they had to exist on nothing but dried figs and mouldy bread, Whoever planned this journey should be ashamed of themselves, the bigwigs at court must think we live on air, he muttered. The men were already striking camp, rolling up blankets and packing away tools, of which there were many, although most would probably never be used, unless the elephant happened to fall down a ravine and had to be winched up. The commanding officer's plan was to set off, with or without the new pair of oxen, as soon as he returned from the village. The sun had now detached itself from the horizon and day had dawned, with only a few clouds floating in the sky, let's just hope it doesn't get so hot that your muscles melt and you feel as if the sweat on your skin was about to come to the boil. The commanding officer summoned the ox-driver, explained what they were going to do and urged him to take a good look at the oxen, assuming there were any, because on them would depend the speed of the expedition and its prompt return to lisbon. The ox-driver said Yes, sir twice, not that he cared, he didn't even live in lisbon, but in a nearby village called mem martins or something of the sort. Since the ox-driver didn't know how to ride a horse, a flagrant example, as you can see, of the negative consequences of over-specialisation, he hoisted himself with some difficulty onto the back of the horse behind the sergeant and off he went, repeating, in a voice that he himself could barely hear, an interminable our father, a prayer of which he was particularly fond because of that bit about forgiving our debts. The problem, and there is always a problem, which sometimes even leaves its tail sticking out just so that we have no illusions about the nature of the beast we're dealing with, comes in the next line, where it says that it is also our duty as christians to forgive our debtors. It just doesn't make sense, it's either one thing or the other, grumbled the ox-driver, if some forgive debts and others don't pay what they owe, where's the profit in that, he wondered. They walked down the first street they came to, although you would need a very vivid imagination to call that path a street, for what it most resembled was a roller coaster, had such things existed then, and the commanding officer asked the first person they met what the name of the village was and where they could find the village's principal landowner. The man, an old peasant carrying his hoe over his shoulder, knew the answers, The principal landowner is the count, but he's not here, The count, repeated the commanding officer, feeling slightly uneasy, Yes, sir, he owns three quarters or more of the land around here, But you say he's not at home, Speak to his steward, sir, he's the captain of the ship, Did you once work at sea, Indeed I did, sir, but the mortality rate was so high, what with drownings and scurvy and other misfortunes, that I resolved to come back home and die on land, And where would I find the steward, If he's not in the fields, he'll be up at the palace, There's a palace here, asked the commanding officer, looking around, It's not one of those tall palaces with towers, it's just two floors, ground floor and first, but they say it holds more treasures than all the mansions and palaces in lisbon, Could you show us the way, asked the commanding officer, That's where I'm heading now, And this count is the count of what. The old man told him, and the commanding officer gave a whistle of amazement, I know him, he said, but I had no idea he owned land hereabouts, And they say he owns land elsewhere too.

The village was of a kind not to be found any more, if it

were winter, it would have been a pigsty awash with water and asquelch with mud, now, though, it reminds one of something else, the petrified ruins of an ancient civilisation, covered in dust, as happens sooner or later to all outdoor museums. They emerged into a square and there was the palace. The old man rang the bell at the service door, and after a minute or so someone opened it and the old man went in. Things were not happening as the commanding officer had imagined, but perhaps it was better that way. The old man would begin negotiations, so to speak, and then it would fall to him to explain precisely why they were there. After a good fifteen minutes, there appeared at the door a fat man sporting a large, droopy moustache resembling nothing so much as a ship's mop. The commanding officer rode over to him and addressed his first words to him from the saddle, just to keep the social demarcations absolutely clear, Are you the count's steward, At your service, sir. The commanding officer then dismounted and, showing unusual astuteness, grasped the words that the steward had presented to him as if on a plate, In that case, serving me and serving the count and his highness the king is all one, If you will be so kind as to explain what you want, sir, and as long as it does not compromise the salvation of my soul or the interests of my master, then I am your man, Neither the interests of your master nor the salvation of your soul will be put at risk by me, I can assure you, but let us get down to the matter that brings me here. He paused, beckoned to the ox-driver to join him and said, I am an officer in the king's cavalry, and the king has charged me with taking to valladolid, in spain, an elephant to be delivered to archduke maximilian of austria, who is currently a guest at the palace of his father-in-law, charles the fifth. The steward's eyes bulged and his mouth dropped open, and the commanding officer made a mental note of both these encouraging signs. Then he went on, We have with us in the convoy an ox-cart to transport bundles of forage for the elephant to eat and a water trough in which he can quench his thirst, now this cart is drawn by a pair of oxen who have, up until now, performed valiantly, but I very much fear that they will not be up to the task when it comes to climbing mountain slopes. The steward nodded, but said nothing. The commanding officer took a deep breath, leaped over a few ornamental phrases he had been lining up in his head and came straight to the point, I need another pair of oxen for the cart and I thought I might find them here, The count is not at home, and only he. The commanding officer interrupted him, You do not seem to have heard what I said, that I am here in the name of the king, it is not I who am asking you for the loan of a pair of oxen for a few days, but his highness the king of portugal, Oh, I heard you, sir, but my master, Is not at home, I know, but his steward is, and he understands his duty to the nation, The nation, sir, Have you never seen it, asked the commanding officer, launching into a lyrical flight of fancy, you see those clouds that know not where they go, they are the nation, you see that sun, which is sometimes there and sometimes not, that is the nation, you see that line of trees, where, with my trousers round my ankles, I first spotted the village this morning, they, too, are the nation, you cannot, therefore, deny me or obstruct my mission, If you say so, sir, My word as a cavalry officer, but enough talk, let us go to the stable and see what oxen you have there. The steward stroked his grubby moustache as if asking its advice, and finally came to a decision, the nation above all else, however, still fearing the consequences of what he was about to do, he asked the officer if he could leave him some kind of guarantee, to which the commanding officer replied, I will leave you a letter written in my own hand in which I will undertake to return the pair of oxen to you as soon as the elephant has been delivered to the archduke of austria, so you will only have to wait for as long as it takes us to travel from here to valladolid and from valladolid to here, Let's go to the stable, then, where we keep the oxen, said the steward, This is my ox-driver, who will come with me, said the commanding officer, for I know more about horses and war, when there is a war. There were eight oxen in the stable. We have another four, said the steward, but they're out in the fields. At a signal from the commanding officer, the ox-driver went over to the animals and examined them closely, one by one, then made two that were lying down stand up, examined them as well, and finally declared, This one and this one, A good choice, they're the best we have, said the steward. The commanding officer felt a wave of pride rise up from his solar plexus to his throat. Every gesture, every step, every decision he made, revealed him to be a strategist of the first water, deserving of the highest recognition and, for a start, swift promotion to the rank of colonel. The steward, who had left the stable, returned with quill and paper, and there the agreement was set down in writing. When the steward received the document, his hands were trembling with excitement, but he calmed down when he heard the ox-driver say, We need harnesses too, They're over there, said the steward. Now, this story has not so far lacked for reflections, of varying degrees of acuity, on human nature, and we have recorded and commented on each one according to their relevance and the mood of the moment. We never expected, however, that one day we would set down such a generous, exalted, sublime thought as that which then passed like lightning through the commanding officer's mind, namely, that to the coat of arms of the count who owned those animals should be added a pair or yoke of oxen, in memory of this event. May that wish be granted. The oxen had been yoked up and the ox-driver was already leading them out of the stable, when the steward asked, And the elephant. Put in this way, as rustic as it was direct, the question could simply have been ignored, but the commanding officer felt that he owed the man a favour, and a feeling akin to gratitude made him say, He's behind those trees, where we spent the night, You know I've never in my life seen an elephant, said the steward sadly, as if his happiness and that of his loved ones depended entirely on him seeing an elephant, Well, we can put that right this minute, come with us, You go on ahead, sir, I'll harness the mule and catch you up. The commanding officer returned to the square, where his sergeant was waiting for him, and he said, Right, we've got the oxen, Yes, sir, they passed by here just now, and the ox-driver looked as pleased as a dog with two tails, Come on then, said the commanding officer, mounting his horse, Yes, sir, said the sergeant, following suit. It did not take them long to reach the rest of their men, and there the commanding officer was faced with a serious dilemma, should he gallop into camp and announce this victory to the assembled hosts or ride alongside the oxen and receive the applause in the presence of that living proof of his ingenuity. It took a good one hundred metres of intense reflection to find an answer to this problem, a solution which, anticipating the term by some five centuries, we might call the third way, and this was to send the sergeant on ahead with the news in order to predispose the men to offer him the most enthusiastic of receptions. And so it was. They had not gone very far when they heard the mule approaching with ungainly step, for the creature had never been required to break into a trot before, still less a gallop. Out of politeness, the commanding officer stopped, as did the sergeant, although he did not know why, and only the ox-driver and the oxen, as if they belonged to another world and were ruled by different laws, continued at their usual pace, that is, a very slow one. The commanding officer gave orders for the sergeant to ride on ahead, but soon regretted having done so. His impatience was growing by the minute. It had been a gross error to send the sergeant on ahead. By then, he would already have received the kind of rapturous applause that always greets good news when given at first hand, and any subsequent applause, however loud, always has a taste of yesterday's warmed-up stew about it. He was wrong. When the commanding officer reached the camp, whether accompanied by or accompanying the ox-driver and the oxen it would be hard to say, the men had formed up into two lines, the labourers on one side, the soldiers on the other, and, in the middle, the elephant with the mahout perched on top, and everyone whooping and applauding wildly, and if this were a pirate ship, it would be the moment to say, A double ration of rum all round. Although this does not preclude the possibility of a quart of red wine being served to the whole company later on. When everyone had calmed down, the convoy began to get itself organised. The ox-driver yoked the count's oxen to the cart, because they were stronger and fresher, and the two that had travelled all the way from lisbon went ahead of them, so that they could rest a little. Whatever the steward may have been thinking, mounted on his mule, he kept crossing himself and then crossing himself again, scarcely able to believe what his eyes were seeing, An elephant, so that's an elephant, he murmured, why, he must be at least four ells high, and then there's the trunk and the tusks and the feet, look how big those feet are. When the convoy set off, he followed it as far as the road. He bade farewell to the commanding officer, to whom he wished a good journey and an even better return, and waved furiously as he watched them move off. Well, it isn't every day that an elephant appears in our lives.

It isn't true that heaven and the heavens are indifferent to our preoccupations and desires. They're constantly sending us signs and warnings, and the only reason we don't add good advice to that list is because experience, heaven's and ours, has shown that memory, which isn't anyone's strong point, is best not overburdened with too much detail. Signs and warnings are easy to interpret if we remain alert, as the commanding officer discovered when, at one point along the route, the convoy was caught in a heavy drenching shower. For the men engaged in the hard work of pushing the ox-cart, that rain was a blessing, an act of charity for the suffering to which the lower classes have always been subject. Solomon and his mahout subhro also enjoyed that sudden cooling rain, although this did not prevent subhro from thinking that, in future, he really could do with an umbrella in such situations, perched up high and unprotected from the water falling from the clouds, especially on the road to vienna. The only ones not to appreciate this atmospheric precipitation were the cavalrymen, proudly got up as usual in their colourful uniforms, now stained and sodden, as if they had just returned, defeated, from a battle. As for their commanding officer, he, with his already proven agility of mind, had understood at once that they were facing a very grave problem. Once again, it just showed that the strategy for this mission had been drawn up by incompetents incapable of foreseeing the most ordinary of eventualities, such as rain in august, when popular wisdom has been warning since time immemorial that winter always begins in august. Unless that shower was a chance occur-

44

rence and the good weather returned for a lengthy period, those nights spent out under the moon or the starry arc of the milky way were over. And that was not all. Having to spend the night in villages meant finding in them a covered area large enough to shelter the horses and the elephant, the four oxen, and several dozen men, and that, as you can imagine, was not easy to find in sixteenth-century portugal, where they had not yet learned to build industrial warehouses or inns for tourists. And what if we get caught in the rain while on the road, not in a shower like this, but in a continuous downpour of the sort that doesn't stop for hours and hours, wondered the commanding officer, concluding, We'll have no option but to get soaked. He looked skywards, scrutinised the heavens and said, It seems to have cleared up for the moment, let's hope it was just a passing threat. Unfortunately, it wasn't. Before they reached safe harbour, if such a description can be applied to a couple of dozen hovels built some distance from each other, and a headless church, that is, one with only half a tower, with not an industrial warehouse to be seen, they met with two more downpours, which the commanding officer, by now an expert in this system of communications, immediately interpreted as two more warnings from the heavens, which had doubtless grown impatient because the necessary preventative measures had not yet been taken to save the rain-drenched convoy from falling victim to colds, chills, flu and doubtless pneumonia. That is the great mistake made by heaven, for whom nothing is impossible, imagining, as it does, that mankind, created, it is said, in the image and likeness of heaven's powerful occupant, enjoys the same privileges. We would like to see what heaven would do in the commanding officer's place, having to go from house to house with the same old story, I'm the officer in charge of a cavalry unit at the service of his highness the king of portugal, our mission being to accompany an elephant to the spanish city of valladolid, and meeting with only distrustful faces, hardly surprising really, given that the people in that part of the world had never even heard of the elephantine species and hadn't the slightest idea what an elephant was. We would like to see heaven asking if there was a large empty barn available or, if not, an industrial warehouse, where both animals and people could shelter for the night, which shouldn't be impossible when one recalls that the famous jesus of galilee, in his prime, boasted of being able to tear down a temple and rebuild it in only three days. We cannot know if the only reason he failed to do so was a lack of manpower or cement, or if he simply reached the sensible conclusion that it wasn't worth the trouble, considering that if he was going to destroy something merely in order to build it up again, it would be better to leave it be. On the other hand, that business with the loaves and fishes really was impressive, and we mention it here only because, by order of the commanding officer and thanks to the efforts of the quartermaster, today there will be hot food for everyone in the convoy, which is no small miracle if one bears in mind the general lack of facilities and the uncertain weather. Luckily, it stopped raining. The men took off their heavier clothes and placed them on poles to dry by the heat of the fires they had lit. Then it was just a matter of waiting for the big pot of stew to arrive and of enjoying the consoling pang in the stomach when they smelled it, knowing that their hunger was finally going to be satisfied, and of feeling just as much a man as those who are brought a plate of food and a slice of bread at regular hours, as if such things were ordained by some beneficent fate. This commanding officer is not like other officers, in that he is as concerned about his men, soldiers and non-soldiers alike, as if they were his children. More than that, he is little concerned with hierarchy, at least in the current circumstances, so much so that he has not gone elsewhere to eat, but is here, taking his place around the fire, and if he hasn't yet participated very much in the conversation, this is only in order to put the men at their ease. One of the cavalrymen has just asked the question that has been preoccupying them all, And what are you going to do with the elephant in vienna, mahout, Probably the same as in lisbon, nothing very much, replied subhro, there'll be a lot of applause, a lot of people crowding the streets, and then they'll forget all about him, that's the law of life, triumph and oblivion, Not always, For elephants and men it is, although I shouldn't really speak of men in general, I'm just an indian in a foreign land, but, as far as I know, only one elephant has ever escaped that law, What elephant was that, asked one of the labourers, An elephant who was dying and whose head was cut off once he was dead, That would be the end of him, then, No, the head was placed on the neck of a god called ganesh, who was also dead, Tell us about this ganesh, said the commanding officer, Sir, the hindu religion is so very complicated that only an indian can really understand it, and even then not always, Now I seem to recall you telling me that you were a christian, And I recall answering, more or less, sir, more or less, What does that mean, though, are you or are you not a christian, Well, I was baptised in india when I was a child, And then, Then, nothing, replied the mahout with a shrug, So you never practised your faith, Sir, I was not called, they must have forgotten about me, You didn't miss anything, said an unknown voice that no one could quite locate, but which, incredible though it may seem, appeared to have come from the embers of the fire. A great silence fell, interrupted only by the crackling of the burning wood. According to your religion, who was it who created the world, asked the commanding officer, Brahma, sir, In other words, god, Yes, but he's not the only god, What do you mean, It's not enough just to have created the world, there has to be someone to preserve it, and that's the job of another god, called vishnu, Are there more gods apart from them, mahout, We've got thousands of them, but the third most important god is shiva, the destroyer, Do you mean that what vishnu preserves shiva destroys, No, sir, with shiva, death is understood as the main creator of life, So, if I understand you correctly, those three gods form part of a trinity, indeed, they are a trinity, just like in christianity, In christianity there are four, sir, if you'll forgive my boldness, Four, exclaimed the commanding officer, astonished, and who's the fourth member, The virgin, sir, The virgin doesn't count, we have the father, the son and the holy ghost, And the virgin, If you don't explain yourself, I'll cut off your head like they did to that elephant, Well, I've never heard anyone ask anything of god or jesus or the holy spirit, but the virgin can barely cope with the torrent of requests and prayers and supplications that arrive at her door at all hours of the day and night, Careful now, the inquisition's out there somewhere, so for your own good, don't go straying into dangerous waters, If I get to vienna, I won't be coming back, Won't you go home to India, asked the commanding officer, No, I'm not an indian any more, And yet you obviously know a lot about hinduism, More or less, sir, more or less,

Why do you say that, Because it's all words and only words, and beyond the words there's nothing, Is ganesh a word, asked the commanding officer, Yes, a word, which, like all the others, can only be explained by more words, but since the words we use to explain things, successfully or not, will, in turn, have to be explained, our conversation will lead nowhere, the mistaken and the true will alternate, like some kind of curse, and we'll never know what's right and what's wrong, Tell me about ganesh, Ganesh is the son of shiva and parvati, who is also known as durga or kali, the goddess of a hundred arms, If she'd had a hundred legs we could have called her centipede, said one of the men with an embarrassed laugh, as if regretting his words as soon as they were out of his mouth. The mahout ignored him and went on, It has to be said that, exactly as happened with your virgin, ganesh was engendered by his mother, parvati, alone, without the intervention of her husband, shiva, who, being eternal, felt no need to have children. One day, when parvati had decided to take a bath, it happened that there were no guards around to protect her should anyone chance to come into the room. And so she created an idol in the form of a little boy, made out of a paste, a kind of soap I suppose, that she herself had prepared. The goddess breathed life into the doll and that was ganesh's first birth. Parvati told ganesh that he must let no one in and he followed his mother's orders to the letter. A short time afterwards, shiva returned from the forest and tried to get into the house, but ganesh wouldn't let him, and that, naturally, made shiva very angry. The following dialogue took place, I'm parvati's husband, therefore her house is my house, Only the people whom my mother wants to come in can enter here, and she did not tell me to let you in. Shiva finally lost patience and

49

launched into a fierce battle with ganesh, which ended with the god cutting off his opponent's head with his trident. When parvati came out and saw the lifeless body of her son, her cries of grief soon became howls of fury. She ordered shiva to bring ganesh back to life at once, but unfortunately, the blow that had decapitated ganesh had been so powerful that his head had been thrown far away and was never seen again. Then, as a last resort, shiva asked for help from brahma, who suggested that he replace ganesh's head with that of the first living being he met on the road, as long as the creature was facing north. Shiva then dispatched his celestial army to go in search of just such a creature. They came across a dying elephant lying with its head to the north and, once it had died, they cut off its head. They returned to shiva and parvati and gave them the elephant's head, which was placed on ganesh's body, thus restoring him to life. And that is how ganesh was born again after having lived and died. Fairy tales, muttered a soldier, Like the one about the man who, having died, rose on the third day, retorted subhro, Careful, mahout, you're going too far, warned the commanding officer, Look, I don't believe in the story about a boy made out of soap who turned into a god with the body of a paunchy man and the head of an elephant, but you asked me to explain who ganesh was, and I did as asked, Yes, but you made some rather rude comments about jesus christ and the virgin that didn't go down at all well with some of the men here, Well, I apologise to anyone who may have felt offended, it was quite unintentional, replied the mahout. There was a conciliatory murmur, and the truth is that those men, both soldiers and civilians, cared little for religious disputes, what troubled them was that such arcane matters should be discussed beneath the celestial vault itself. They say that walls have ears, well, imagine the size of the stars' ears. Anyway, it was time to go to bed, even though the sheets and blankets were the clothes they had worn during the day, the main thing was that they wouldn't get rained on, and the commanding officer had achieved precisely this by going from house to house asking the residents if they would be prepared to provide shelter that night for a few of his men, who thus ended up sleeping in kitchens, stables and haylofts, but this time with a full belly, which made up for these and other inconveniences. With them went a few villagers, too, most of them men, who had walked over to the camp, attracted by the novelty of seeing an elephant, although, out of fear, they dared not approach nearer than twenty paces. Coiling his trunk around a bundle of forage that would have been enough to take the edge off the appetite of a squadron of cows, solomon, despite his poor sight, shot them a stern glance, making it clear that he was not some fairground animal, but an honest worker who had been deprived of his job by unfortunate circumstances too complicated to go into, and had, so to speak, been forced to accept public charity. At first, one of the village men, out of bravado, went a few steps beyond the invisible line that would soon become a closed frontier, but solomon shooed him away with a warning kick, which, even though it didn't hit its target, gave rise to an interesting debate among the men about animal families and clans. John mules and molly mules, jacks and jennies, stallions and mares, are all quadrupeds who, as everyone knows, some by painful experience, can deliver a kick, and that's perfectly understandable, since they have no other weapons, either offensive or defensive, but an elephant, with that trunk and those tusks, with those huge great legs that look like

51

steam-hammers, can also, as if this weren't enough, kick with the best of them. He may appear to be mildness incarnate, but, when necessary, he can turn into a wild beast. It's odd, though, that, belonging as he does to the aforementioned family of animals, namely, the family that kicks, he doesn't wear horseshoes. One of the villagers said, There's not much to an elephant really. The others agreed, When you've walked round him once, you've seen all there is to see. They could have returned to their homes then, but one of them said he was going to stay a little longer, that he wanted to hear what was being talked about around the fire. His companions went with him. At first, they couldn't understand what the topic of conversation was, they couldn't catch the names, which had strange pronunciations, then all became clear when they reached the conclusion that these men were talking about the elephant and that the elephant was god. They were walking back to their houses now, to the comfort of their own hearth, each one taking with him two or three guests, both soldiers and labourers. Two cavalrymen stayed behind to guard the elephant, which reinforced in the villagers the idea that they needed to talk to the priest urgently. The doors closed and the village shrank into the darkness. Shortly afterwards, a few of those doors swung cautiously open again, and the five men who emerged from them set off for the well in the square, where they had agreed to meet. They had decided to go and talk to the priest, who would, at that hour, doubtless be asleep in his bed. The priest was known to have a foul temper if woken at an inconvenient hour, and that, for him, was any hour during which he was safe in the arms of morpheus. One of the men suggested an alternative, Why don't we come back in the morning, he asked, but another, more determined, or simply more susceptible to the logic of caution, objected, If they've decided to leave at dawn, we risk finding no one, and then we'll look a right bunch of fools. They were standing at the gate to the priest's garden, and it seemed that none of the night visitors dared lift the knocker. There was also a knocker on the door of the priest's house, but it was too small to wake the inhabitant. Finally, like a cannon shot in the stony silence of the village, the knocker on the garden gate boomed into life. They had to knock twice more before they heard, coming from within, the hoarse, angry voice of the priest, Who is it. Obviously, it was neither prudent nor comfortable to talk about god in the middle of the street, with thick walls and a heavy wooden door between the two parties to the conversation. It would not be long before the neighbours were pricking up their ears to listen to the loud voices in which both sides of the dialogue would be obliged to speak, transforming a very serious theological matter into the latest piece of gossip. The door of the house finally opened and the priest's round head appeared, What do you want at this hour of the night. The men left the other door and walked reluctantly up the path to the house. Is someone dying, asked the priest. They all said No, sir. So what is it then, insisted this servant of god, drawing the blanket covering his shoulders more tightly about him, We can't talk out here in the street, said one of the men. The priest grumbled, Well, if you can't talk in the street, come to the church tomorrow, We have to talk to you now, father, tomorrow might be too late, the matter that brings us here is very serious, a church matter, A church matter, repeated the priest, suddenly uneasy, thinking that one of the church's rotten ceiling beams must finally have given way, Come in, then, come in. He herded them into the kitchen, where a few logs were still glowing in the hearth, then he lit a candle, sat down on a stool and said, Speak. The men looked at one another, unsure who should be the spokesman, but it was clear that the only legitimate candidate was the one who had said he was going to listen to what was being discussed in the group that included the commanding officer and the mahout. No vote was necessary, the man in question took the floor, God is an elephant, father. The priest gave a sigh of relief, this was certainly preferable to the roof falling in, what's more, the heretical statement was easy enough to answer, God is in all his creatures, he said. The men nodded, but the spokesman, conscious of his rights and responsibilities, retorted, But none of them is god, That's all we'd need, replied the priest, the world would be bursting with gods then, and they'd never agree, each one trying to heap up the coals beneath his particular pot, Father, what we heard, with these ears that will one day be dust, is that the elephant over there is god, Who said such an outlandish thing, asked the priest, using a word that wasn't common currency in the village, and this, in him, was a clear sign that he was angered, The cavalry officer and the man who rides on top, On top of what, Of god, of the animal. The priest took a deep breath and, suppressing the urge to take more extreme measures, merely said, You're drunk, No, father, they replied in chorus, it's really quite difficult to get drunk these days, what with the price of wine, Well, if you're not drunk, and if despite this cock-and-bull story, you're still good christians, listen to me closely. The men drew nearer so as not to miss a word, and the priest, having first cleared his throat of catarrh, the result, he thought, of being dragged so abruptly from his warm sheets into the cold outside world, launched into a sermon, I could send you home with a penance, a few our fathers and a few hail marys, and think no more of the matter, but since you seem to me men of good faith, tomorrow morning, before the sun is up, we will all go, along with your families and the other villagers, whom I leave it up to you to tell, to find this elephant, not in order to excommunicate him, since, being an animal, he has never received the holy sacrament of baptism nor could he ever have enjoyed the spiritual benefits granted by the church, but in order to cleanse him of any diabolical possession that may have been introduced into his brute nature by the evil one, as happened to those two thousand swine that drowned in the sea of galilee, as I'm sure you'll remember. He paused, then asked, Understood, Yes, father, they replied, all except the spokesman who was clearly taking his role very seriously indeed, Father, he said, I always found that story most puzzling, Why, Well, I don't understand why those swine had to die, it's good that jesus performed the miracle of driving out the unclean spirits from the body of the gadarene demoniac, but letting those spirits then enter the bodies of a few poor creatures who had nothing to do with the matter never seemed to me a good way of finishing the task, especially since demons are immortal, because if they weren't, god would have killed them off at birth, what I mean is that by the time the pigs had fallen in the water, the demons would have escaped anyway, and it just seems to me that jesus didn't really think it through, And who are you to say that jesus didn't really think it through, It's written down, father, But you don't know how to read, Ah, but I know how to listen, Is there a bible in your house, No, father, only the gospels, they were part of a bible, but someone tore them out, And who reads them, My eldest daughter, she can't read very quickly yet, but she's read the same thing to us over and over now and we're beginning to understand it better, The trouble is that if the inquisition were ever to hear that you held such ideas and opinions, you'd be the first to be consigned to the flames, Well, we all have to die of something, father, Don't talk such nonsense, leave your gospels and pay more attention to what I say in church, indicating the right path is my mission and no one else's, just remember, better to go the long way round than fall into a ditch, Yes, father, And not a word about what's been said here, if anyone outside of this group ever mentions the matter to me, then the one of you who let his tongue wag will be instantly excommunicated, even if I have to go to rome myself to give personal testimony. He paused for dramatic effect, and then asked in a portentous voice, Do you understand, Yes, father, we understand, Tomorrow, before the sun comes up, I want everyone gathered outside the church, I, your pastor, will go in front, and together, with my word and your presence, we will fight for our holy religion, and just remember, the people united will never be defeated.

The dawn was a foggy one, but despite a mist almost as thick as a soup made solely of boiled potatoes, no one had got lost, everyone had found their way to the church just as the guests to whom the villagers had given shelter had found their way back to the encampment earlier. The whole village was there, from the tiniest babe-in-arms to the oldest man still capable of walking, thanks to the aid of a stick that functioned as his third leg. Fortunately, he didn't have as many legs as a centipede, for centipedes, when they get old, require an enormous number of sticks, a fact that tips the scales in favour of the human species, who need only one, except in the very gravest of cases, when the afore-mentioned sticks change their name and become crutches. Of these, thanks to the divine providence that watches over us all, there were none in the village. The column was advancing at a steady pace, screwing up its courage in readiness to write a new page of selfless heroism in the annals of the village, the other pages not having much to offer the erudite reader, only that we were born, we worked and we died. Almost all the women had come armed with their rosaries and were murmuring prayers, doubtless in order to strengthen the resolve of the priest, who walked in front, bearing an aspergillum and a container of holy water. Now because of the mist, the men in the convoy had not yet dispersed as would have been natural, but were waiting in small groups to be given their usual breakfast chunk of bread, including the soldiers, who, being earlier risers, had already harnessed the horses. When the villagers began to emerge from the potato soup, the people in charge of the elephant instinctively went forward to meet them, with the cavalrymen in the vanguard, as was their duty. When the two groups were within hailing distance, the priest stopped, raised his hand in a sign of peace, said good morning and asked, Where is the elephant, we want to see it. The sergeant considered both question and request quite reasonable and replied, Behind those trees, although if you want to see him, you'll have to speak first to the commanding officer and the mahout, What's a mahout, The man who rides on top, On top of what, On top of the elephant, what do you think, So mahout means the person who goes on top, Search me, I've no idea what it means, all I know is that he rides on top, it's an indian word apparently. This conversation would have looked set to continue for some time in this vein had not the commanding officer and the mahout approached, attracted by the curious sight, glimpsed through the now slightly thinning mist, of what could have been two armies face to face. Here's the commanding officer now, said the sergeant, glad to be able to leave a conversation that was already beginning to get on his nerves. The commanding officer said, Good morning, then asked, How may I help you, We would like to see the elephant, It really isn't the best moment, said the mahout, he's a bit grumpy when he wakes up. To which the priest responded, As well as seeing the elephant, my flock and I would like to bless him before he sets off on his long journey, which is why I've brought the aspergillum and the holy water, That's a very nice idea, said the commanding officer, none of the other priests we've met along the way so far has offered to bless solomon, Who's solomon, asked the priest, The elephant's name is solomon, replied the mahout, It doesn't seem right to me to give an animal the name of a person, animals aren't people and people aren't animals, Well, I'm not so sure, said the mahout, who was starting to get fed up with all this blather, That's the difference between those who are educated and those who are not, retorted the priest with reprehensible arrogance. And with that, he turned to the commanding officer and asked, Would you allow me, sir, to do my duty as a priest, That's fine by me, father, although I'm not the person in charge of the elephant, that's the mahout's job. Instead of waiting for the priest to address him, subhro said in suspiciously friendly tones, Please, father, solomon is all yours. It is time to warn the reader that two of the characters here are not acting in good faith. First and foremost, there is the priest, who, contrary to what he said, has not brought with him holy water, but water from the well, taken directly from the jug in the kitchen, without ever having been touched by the empyrean, not even symbolically, secondly, there is the mahout, who is hoping something will happen and is praying to the god ganesh that it does. Don't get too close, warned the commanding officer, he's three metres high and weighs about four tons, if not more, He can't be as dangerous as the leviathan, a beast that has been subjugated for ever by the holy catholic and apostolic roman church to which I belong, The responsibility is yours, but I've given you due warning, said the commanding officer, who, during his time as a soldier, had listened to many brave boasts and witnessed the sad outcome of almost all of them. The priest dipped the aspergillum in the water, took three steps forward and sprinkled the elephant's head with it, at the same time murmuring words that sounded like latin, although no one understood them, not even the tiny educated minority present, namely, the commanding officer, who had spent some years in a seminary, the result of a mystical crisis that eventually cured itself. The priest continued his murmurings and gradually worked his way round to the other end of the animal, a movement that coincided with a rapid increase in the mahout's prayers to the god ganesh and the sudden realisation on the part of the commanding officer that the priest's words and gestures belonged to the manual of exorcism, as if the poor elephant could possibly be possessed by a demon. The man's mad, the commanding officer thought, and in the very instant in which he thought this, he saw the priest thrown to the ground, with the holy water container to one side, the aspergillum to the other, and the water spilled. The flock rushed to help their pastor, but the soldiers stepped in to avoid people getting crushed in the confusion, and quite right too, because the priest, helped by the village titans, was already trying to get up and had clearly sustained an injury to his left hip, although everything indicated that no bones were broken, which, bearing in mind his advanced age and his stout, flabby body, could almost be considered one of the most remarkable miracles ever performed by the local patron saint. What really happened, and we will never know why, yet another inexplicable mystery to add to all the others, was that solomon, when he was less than a span or so from the target of the tremendous kick he was about to unleash, held back and softened the blow, so that the effects were only those that might result from a hard shove, but not a deliberate one and certainly not one intended to kill. Lacking that important piece of information, the dazed priest merely kept repeating, It was a punishment from heaven, a punishment from heaven. From that day on, whenever anyone mentions elephants in his presence, and this must have happened many times given what occurred here, on this misty morning, with so many witnesses present, he will always say that these apparently brutish animals are, in fact, so intelligent that, as well as having a smattering of latin, they are also capable of distinguishing ordinary water from holy water. The priest let himself be led, limping, to the rosewood chair, a magnificent piece of joinery almost worthy of an abbot's throne, that four of his most devoted followers had run to the church to fetch. We will not be here when they finally return to the village. The discussion will be a stormy one, as is only to be expected among people not much given to exercising their reason, men and women who come to blows over the slightest thing, even when, as in this case, they are trying to decide on the pious task of how best to carry their pastor back to his house and put him to bed. The priest will not be of much help in settling the dispute because he will fall into a torpor that will be a cause of great concern to everyone, except the local witch, Don't worry, she said, there are no signs of imminent death, not today or tomorrow, and nothing that can't be put right by a few vigorous massages of the affected parts and some herbal tea to purify the blood and avoid corruption, meanwhile, stop this bickering, it will only end in tears, all you need do is to take turns carrying him and change places every fifty paces, that way friendship will prevail. And the witch was quite right.

The convoy of men, horses, oxen and elephant has been swallowed up by the mist, so that you cannot even make out the vast general shape of them. We'll have to run to catch them up. Fortunately, considering the brief time we spent listening to the village titans' arguments, the convoy won't have gone very far. In normal visibility or when the mist bore less of a resemblance to potato purée, we would only have to follow the tracks left in the soft soil by the thick wheels of the ox-cart and the quartermaster's wagon, but, now, even with your nose pressed to the ground, you still wouldn't be able to tell if anyone had passed. And not just people, but animals too, some of considerable size, like the oxen and the horses, and, in particular, the pachyderm known in the portuguese court as solomon, whose feet would leave in the earth enormous almost circular footprints, like those of the round-footed dinosaurs, if they ever existed. And speaking of animals, it seems impossible that no one in lisbon thought to bring a few dogs with them. A dog is a life insurance policy, a tracker of noises, a four-legged compass. You would just have to say to it, Fetch, and in less than five

61

minutes, it would be back, tail wagging and eyes shining with happiness. There is no wind, although the mist seems to form slow whirlpools as if boreas himself were blowing it down from the far north, from the lands of eternal ice. However, to be honest, given the delicacy of the situation, this is hardly the moment for someone to be honing his prose in order to make some, frankly, not very original poetic point. By now, the people travelling with the caravan will have realised that someone is missing, indeed two of them will probably have volunteered to go and save the poor cast-away, an action that would be most welcome if it weren't for the reputation as a coward that will follow the castaway for the rest of his days, Honestly, the public voice will say, imagine him just sitting there, waiting for someone to rescue him, some people have no shame at all. It's true that he had been sitting down, but now he's standing up and has cour-ageously taken the first step, right foot first, to drive away the evil spells cast by fate and its powerful allies, chance and coincidence, however, his left foot has grown suddenly hesi-tant, and who can blame it, because the ground is invisible, as if a new tide of mist had just begun to roll in. With his third step, he can no longer see his own hands held out in front of him as if to keep his nose from bumping against some unexpected door. It was then that another idea occurred to him, what if the road curved this way and that, and the direction he had taken, in what he hoped would be a straight line, led him into desert places that would mean perdition for both soul and body, in the case of the latter with imme-diate effect. And, o unhappy fate, without even a dog to lick away his tears when the great moment arrived. He again considered turning back to ask for shelter in the village until the bank of mist lifted of its own accord, but now, completely disoriented, with as little idea of where the cardinal points might be as if he were in some entirely unfamiliar place, he decided that his best bet was to sit down on the ground again and wait for destiny, chance, fate, any or all of them together, to guide those selfless volunteers to the tiny patch of ground on which he was sitting, as on an island in the ocean sea, with no means of communication. Or, more appropriately, like a needle in a haystack. Within three minutes, he was fast asleep. What a strange creature man is, so prone to terrible insomnias over mere nothings and yet capable of sleeping like a log on the eve of a battle. And so it was. He fell into a deep sleep, and it's quite likely that he would still be sleeping now if, somewhere in the mist, solomon had not unleashed a thunderous trumpeting whose echoes must have been heard on the distant shores of the ganges. Still groggy after his abrupt awakening, he could not make out precisely where it was coming from, that fog horn come to save him from an icy death or, worse, from being eaten by wolves, because this is a land of wolves, and a man, alone and unarmed, is helpless against a whole pack of them or, indeed, against one. Solomon's second blast was even louder than the first and began with a kind of quiet gurgling in the depths of his throat, like a roll on the drums, immediately followed by the syncopated clamour that typifies the creature's call. The man is now racing through the mist like a horseman charging, lance at the ready, thinking all the while, Again, solomon, again. And solomon granted his wish and let out another trumpet blast, quieter this time, as if merely confirming that he was there, because the castaway is no longer adrift, he's on his way, there's the wagon belonging to the cavalry quartermaster, not that he can make out details because things and people are nothing but blurs, it's as if the mist, and this is a much more troubling idea, were of a kind that can corrode the skin, the skin of people, horses, even elephants, yes, even that vast, tiger-proof elephant, not all mists are the same, of course, one day, someone will cry Gas, and woe betide anyone not wearing a tight-fitting mask. The ex-castaway asks a soldier who happens to be passing, leading his horse by the reins, if the volunteers have returned from their rescue mission, and the soldier responds with a distrustful glance, as if he were speaking to some kind of provocateur, because, as a quick flick through the inquisition's files will confirm, there were plenty of them around in the sixteenth century, and says coolly, Wherever did you get an idea like that, there was no call for volunteers here, the only sensible course of action in a situation like this is to do exactly as we did and sit tight until the mist lifts, besides, asking for volunteers isn't really the captain's style, usually, he just points, you, you and you, quick march, and anyway, the captain says that when it comes to heroics, either all of us are going to be heroes or none. To make clearer still that he considered the conversation to be at an end, the soldier rapidly hoisted himself up onto his horse, said goodbye and galloped off into the mist. He was displeased with himself. He had given explanations that no one had asked him for, and made statements he was not authorised to make. However, he was consoled by the fact that the man, although he didn't really have the physique, probably belonged, what other possibility was there, to the group of men hired to help push or pull the ox-carts whenever the going got rough, men of few words and even less imagination. Generally speaking, that is, because the man lost in the mist certainly didn't appear to lack imagination, just look at the way he had plucked out of nothing, out of nowhere, the volunteers who should have come to his rescue. Fortunately for the man's public credibility, the elephant is a different matter altogether. Large, enormous, big-bellied, with a voice guaranteed to terrify the timid and a trunk like that of no other animal in creation, the elephant could never be the product of anyone's imagination, however bold and fertile. The elephant either existed or it didn't. It is, there-fore, time to visit him and thank him for the energetic way in which he used his god-given trumpet to such good purpose, for if this had been the valley of jehoshaphat, the dead would undoubtedly have risen again, but being what it is, an ordinary scrap of Portuguese earth swathed in mist where someone very nearly died of cold and indifference, and so as not entirely to waste the rather laboured compar-ison with which we chose to encumber ourselves, we might say that some resurrections are so deftly handled that they can happen even before the poor victim has passed away. It was as if the elephant had thought, That poor devil is going to die, and I'm going to save him. And here's the same poor devil heaping thanks on him and swearing eternal gratitude, until finally the mahout asks, What did the elephant do to deserve such thanks, If it wasn't for him, I would have died of cold or been devoured by wolves, And what exactly did he do, because he hasn't left this spot since he woke up, He didn't need to move, he just had to blow his trumpet, because I was lost in the mist and it was his voice that saved me, If anyone is qualified to speak of the works and deeds of solomon, I'm that man, which is why I'm his mahout, so don't come to me with some story about hearing him trumpet, He didn't just trumpet once, but three times, and these same ears that will one day be dust heard him trumpet. The mahout thought, The fellow's stark staring mad, the mist must have seeped into his brain, that's probably it, yes, I've heard of such cases, then, out loud he added, Let's not argue about whether it was one, two or three blasts, you ask those men over there if they heard anything. The men, whose blurred outlines seemed to vibrate and tremble with every step, immediately gave rise to the question, Where are you off to in weather like this. We know, however, that this wasn't the question asked by the man who insisted he'd heard the elephant speak and we know the answer they were giving him. What we don't know is whether any of these things are related, which ones, or how. The fact is that the sun, like a vast broom of light, suddenly broke through the mist and swept it away. The landscape revealed itself as it had always been, stones, trees, ravines, and mountains. The three men are no longer there. The mahout opens his mouth to speak, then closes it again. The man who insisted he'd heard the elephant speak began to lose consistency and substance, to shrink, then grow round and transparent as a soap bubble, if the poor-quality soaps of the time were capable of forming the crystalline marvels that someone had the genius to invent, then he suddenly disappeared from view. He went plof and vanished. Onomatopoeia can be so very handy. Imagine if we'd had to provide a detailed description of someone disappearing. It would have taken us at least ten pages. Plof.

By chance, perhaps as the result of some change in the atmosphere, the commanding officer found himself thinking about his wife and children, she five months pregnant and they, a boy and a girl, six and four years old respectively. The primitive people of the time, barely emerged from primæval barbarism, pay so little attention to delicate feelings that they rarely make use of them. Certain emotions may already be fermenting away in the laborious process of creating a coherent and cohesive national identity, but that quintessentially portuguese feeling of yearning and nostalgia known as *saudade*, and all its by-products, had not yet been embraced by portugal as a habitual philosophy of life, and this has given rise to not a few communication difficulties in society in general and to some degree of perplexity on a personal level as well. For example, basic common sense tells us that it would be inadvisable to go over to the commanding officer now and ask, Tell me, sir, would you describe what you feel for your wife and your little children as *saudade*. The officer, although not entirely lacking in taste and sensibility, as we have had the opportunity to observe already at various points in this story, although always maintaining the utmost discretion so as not to offend against the character's natural modesty, would stare at us, astonished by our patent lack of tact and give us some vague and airy answer, neither here nor there, that would leave us, at the very least, with serious concerns about the couple's private life. It's true that the commanding officer has never sung a serenade nor, as far as we know, written a single sonnet, but that doesn't mean that he is not, by nature shall we say, perfectly capable of appreciating the beautiful things created by his ingenious fellow creatures. One of these, for example, he could have brought with him in his knapsack, carefully swathed in cloth, as he had done on other more war-like expeditions, but this time he had chosen to leave it safely at home. Given how little money he earns, an amount, often paid in arrears, that was evidently not intended by the treasury to allow the troops to enjoy any luxuries, the commanding officer, in order to purchase his particular jewel, a good twelve or more years ago now, had to sell a baldric made of the finest materials, delicate in design and richly decorated, intended, it's true, to be worn more in the drawing-room than on the battlefield, a magnificent piece of military equipment that had been the property of his maternal grandfather and which, ever since, had been an object of desire for whoever laid eyes on it. In its place, but not intended for the same ends, is a large volume bearing the title amadis of gaul, whose author, as certain of our more patriotic scholars claim, was a certain vasco de lobeira, a portuguese writer of the fourteenth century, whose work was published in zaragoza, in fifteen hundred and eight, in a castilian translation by one garci rodriguez de montalvo, who besides adding a few extra chapters of love and adventure, also amended and corrected the original texts. The commanding officer suspects that his copy is of bastard stock, what we would call a pirate edition, which just goes to show how long certain illicit commercial practices have been going on. Solomon, and we are speaking here of the king of judah and not the elephant, was quite right when he wrote that there was nothing new under the sun. It's hard for us to imagine that in those biblical times everything was much the same as it is now, for our stubborn innocence insists on imagining them as lyrical, bucolic, pastoral, perhaps because they are still so close to our own first fumbling attempts at creating our western civilisation.

The commanding officer is on his fourth or fifth reading of amadis. As in any other chivalric novel, there is no shortage of bloody battles, with arms and legs lopped off at the root and bodies sliced in two, which says a great deal for the brute force of those spiritual knights, given that the cutting virtues of metal alloys made of vanadium and molybdenum, to be found nowadays in any ordinary kitchen knife, were unknown then, indeed unimaginable, which just goes to show how far we have progressed, and in the right direction too. The book recounts in pleasurable detail the troubled loves of amadis of gaul and oriana, both of whom were the children of kings, although this did not prevent amadis being abandoned by his mother, who gave orders that he be placed in a wooden box, with a sword beside him, and put to sea, at the mercy of the maritime currents and the force of the waves. As for oriana, poor thing, she found herself, against her will, promised in marriage by her own father to the emperor of rome, when she had placed all her desires and hopes in amadis, whom she had loved since she was seven and he was twelve, although physically he looked more like a fifteen-year-old. Seeing each other and falling in love had taken but one dazzling moment that continued to dazzle them all their lives. This was a time when knights errant had pledged to complete god's work and eliminate evil from the planet. It was also a time when love was only deemed to be love if it was of an extreme and radical nature, when absolute fidelity was a spiritual gift as natural as eating and drinking are to the body. And speaking of bodies, it is worth pondering just what state amadis' body would have been in, covered in scars as it was, when he embraced the perfect body of the peerless oriana. Armour, without the help of molybdenum and vanadium, would be of little use, and the narrator of the story makes no attempt to disguise the frailty of corslets and coats of mail. A simple blow with a sword was enough to render a helmet useless and to split open the head inside. It's astonishing that those people survived into the present century. That's what I'd like to do, sighed the commanding officer. He wouldn't mind giving up the rank of captain, at least for a while, in exchange for setting out on horseback, like a new amadis of gaul, along the beaches of ilha firme or through the woods and mountains where the enemies of the lord were hiding. In times of peace, the life of a portuguese cavalry captain is one of complete idleness, and you really have to rack your brains to find something with which you can usefully occupy the empty hours of the day. The captain imagines amadis riding through the rugged countryside, with the pitiless stones punishing his horse's hooves and his squire gandalim telling his friend that it is time to rest. This fantastical wish caused the captain's thoughts to deviate onto an entirely non-literary matter to do with the most basic rules of military discipline, that of carrying out orders. If the commanding officer had been able to enter into the cogitations of king dom joão the third at the moment we described earlier, when that royal personage imagined solomon and his entourage crossing the vast, monotonous lands of castile, he would not be here now, going up and down these ravines, dodging dangerous slopes, while the ox-driver tries to find paths that do not take him too far out of his way whenever the incipient and ill-defined tracks disappear beneath rubble and shale. Although the king did not actually express an opinion and no one dared ask him to opine on such a trivial matter, the general of the cavalry gave his approval, yes, the route across the plains of castile was definitely the best and the easiest, almost, one might say, a stroll in the country. This, then, was how things stood, and there would, it seemed, have been no reason to reconsider the itinerary had the king's secretary, pêro de alcáçova carneiro, not happened to learn of this agreement and decided to intervene. What you are calling a stroll in the country, sir, is not, I feel, a good idea, he said, if we're not very careful, it could have negative consequences of a serious, even grave nature, Well, I don't see why, What if we should meet with difficulties in obtaining food or water supplies from the local population while we're crossing castile, what if the people there refuse to do business with us, even though that goes against their own best interests at the time, That is a possibility, agreed the general, What if bandits, far more numerous there than here, seeing the meagre protection given to the elephant, because, after all, a troop of thirty cavalrymen is nothing, Now there I must disagree with you, sir, the general broke in, if there had been thirty portuguese soldiers at thermopylae, for example, on whichever side, the battle would have turned out quite differently, Forgive me, sir, it was certainly not my intention to cast doubt upon the bravery of our glorious army, but, as I was saying, what if those bandits, who doubtless know the value of ivory, were to join forces and attack us, kill the elephant and tear out his tusks, Some claim that the hide of an elephant is impermeable to bullets, That may be true, but there would certainly be other ways of killing him, what I'm asking your majesty to consider, above all,

71

is the shame that would befall us if we lost our gift to arch-duke maximilian in a skirmish with spanish bandits and on spanish territory, So what do you think we should do then, There is only one alternative to the castile route, our own, along the frontier, heading north, as far as castelo rodrigo, Those are very bad roads, said the general, you clearly don't know the area, No, but we have no other option, and it does bring with it another advantage, Which is, That of being able to make most of the journey on portuguese soil, An important detail, no doubt about it, you think of every-thing, secretary.

Two weeks after this conversation, it became evident that the secretary, pêro de alcáçova carneiro, had not, in fact, thought of everything. A messenger from the archduke's secretary arrived bearing a letter in which, amongst other trifles that seemed to have been deliberately included in order to distract the reader's attention, he asked precisely where on the frontier the elephant would cross, because a detachment of spanish or austrian soldiers would be there to receive him. The portuguese secretary replied through the same messenger, informing him that they would cross the frontier at castelo rodrigo, and then he immediately launched a counter-attack. Now while such an expression may seem a gross exaggeration, bearing in mind that peace reigns between the two iberian countries, pêro de alcáçova carneiro's sixth sense had reared up at the word used by his spanish colleague, receive. The man could have used such words as greet or welcome, but no, he had either said more than he intended or, as they say, the truth had slipped out by mistake. A few instructions to the cavalry captain on how to proceed will avoid any misunderstandings, thought pêro de alcáçova carneiro, if the other side is of the same mind. The result of this strategic planning is being announced by the sergeant, in another place and a few days later, at this very moment, There are two horsemen behind us, sir. The commanding officer looked at the approaching horses, which were obviously thoroughbreds judging by their long stride and their speed, and they were clearly in a hurry. The sergeant had ordered the column to halt, and just in case, made sure that a few muskets were kept discreetly trained on the new arrivals. Limbs shaking and foam dripping from their mouths, the horses were breathing hard when they came to a stop. The two riders greeted the officer and one of them said, We come bearing a message from secretary pêro de alcáçova carneiro for the commanding officer of the troops accompanying the elephant, I am that commanding officer. The man opened his knapsack and took out a piece of paper folded in four and sealed with the official stamp of the king's secretary, then handed it to the commanding officer, who moved a few paces away in order to read it. When he rejoined them, his eyes were shining. He called the sergeant to one side and said, Sergeant, tell the quartermaster to give these men some food and prepare them some provisions for the journey back, Yes, sir, And announce that the time allowed today for the afternoon rest will be reduced by half, Yes, sir, We have to reach castelo rodrigo before the spanish do, which should be possible, since they, unlike us, have not been forewarned, And if we don't, sir, the sergeant made so bold as to ask, We will, but anyway, the first to arrive will have to wait. As simple as that, the first to arrive will have to wait, it hardly seemed worth pêro de alcáçova carneiro writing such a letter. There must be more to it than that.

The wolves appeared the following day. Perhaps they had heard us mention them earlier and finally decided to show up. They don't appear to have come in a spirit of war, possibly because the results of their hunting during the latter part of the night were enough to fill their stomachs, besides, a convoy like this of more than fifty men, many of them armed, instils a certain sense of respect and prudence, wolves might be bad, but they're not stupid. They're experts at weighing up the relative strength of the forces involved on either side and never let themselves be carried away by enthusiasm, never lose their heads, perhaps because they have no flag or military band to sweep them to glory, no, when they launch an attack, they do so in order to win, a rule to which, however, as we will see later on, there is the occasional exception. These wolves had never seen an elephant. It would not surprise us to learn that some of the more imaginative wolves, always assuming wolves have thought processes parallel to those of human beings, had thought how lucky it would be for the pack to have at its disposal all those tons of meat just outside the lair, the table always set for lunch, dinner and supper. The ingenuous canis lupus signatus, the latin name of the iberian wolf, does not know that the elephant's skin is impervious to bullets, although one must, of course, bear in mind the enormous difference between old-fashioned bullets, which you could never be sure would go precisely where you wanted them to, and the teeth of these three representatives of the lupine race gazing down from the top of a hill at the lively spectacle of that column of men, horses and oxen preparing for the next stage of their journey to castelo rodrigo. It's quite possible that solomon's skin would not have resisted for long the concerted action of three lots of very sharp teeth honed over the centuries by the need to survive and to eat absolutely anything that crossed their path. The men are talking about the wolves, and one of them says to those nearby, If you're ever attacked by a wolf and all you have is a stick to defend yourself with, on no account let the wolf get his teeth round it, Why, asked someone, Because the wolf will gradually work his way up the stick, all the time keeping a firm grip on the wood, until he's close enough to pounce, Devilish creatures, To be fair, though, wolves are not the natural enemies of man, and if they sometimes appear to be, that's only because we're an obstacle to their having a free run of everything the world has to offer an honest wolf, Those three don't look as if they harbour any particularly hostile intentions, They must have eaten already, besides there are too many of us for them to dare to attack, say, one of those horses, which for them would be a very tasty morsel indeed, There they go, shouted a soldier. It was true. The wolves, who, from the moment they arrived, had been sitting utterly motionless, silhouetted against the backdrop of clouds, were now moving off, as if gliding rather than walking, until they disappeared, one by one. Will they be back, asked the soldier, Possibly, perhaps just to see whether or not we're still here or if an injured horse has been left behind, said the man who knew about wolves. Up ahead, the bugle sounded the order to assemble. More or less half an hour later, the column lumbered into action, with the ox-cart at the front, followed by the elephant and the porters, then the cavalry and, bringing up the rear, the quartermaster's wagon. They

75

were all exhausted. Meanwhile, the mahout had informed the commanding officer that solomon was tired, not so much because of the distance they had travelled from lisbon, but because of the terrible state of the roads, if they merited that name. The commanding officer informed him that in a day or, at most, two, they would be within sight of castelo rodrigo, If we arrive first, he added, the elephant will be able to rest for however many days or hours it takes for the spanish to join us, as will everyone else in our party, men and beasts, And what if we arrive after them, That depends on how much of a hurry they're in and what their orders are, although I imagine that they, too, will want at least one day's repose, We're in your hands, sir, and my one desire is that your interests might also be our interests, They are, said the commanding officer. He dug in his spurs and rode on ahead, to encourage the ox-driver, for the speed of the convoy's progress depended in large measure on his driving skills, Come on, man, get those oxen moving, he shouted, it's not far to castelo rodrigo now and it won't be long before we can sleep under a roof again, And eat like human beings, I hope, said the ox-driver in a low murmur so that no one would hear him. At any rate, the commanding officer's orders did not fall on deaf ears. The driver used his prod to urge the oxen on, then shouted a few words of encouragement in that dialect common to all ox-drivers, with immediate and effective results, an impetus that was maintained for the next ten minutes or quarter of an hour, or for as long as the ox-driver could keep the flame burning. Feeling more dead than alive, starving but too weary to eat, the convoy pitched camp when the sun had already set and night was upon them. Fortunately, the wolves had not come back. If they had, they would have been able to saunter round half the encampment and choose the most succulent victim from among the horses. True, such a grandiose theft would have come to no good, a horse being too large an animal to be dragged off just like that, but if they had succeeded, we would not have found words strong enough to describe the travellers' fear when they realised that wolves had infiltrated the camp, and it would be a matter then of every man for himself. Let us give thanks to heaven that we were spared that test. Let us also thank heaven that the imposing towers of the castle have just come into view, it makes one feel like saying, as someone else once did, Today you will be with me in paradise, or, to use the commanding officer's more down-to-earth words, Tonight we'll sleep under a roof, but then, no two paradises are alike, some have houris and some do not, however, to find out just what kind of paradise we're in, all we need do is peer round the door. With a wall to protect you from the cold north wind, a roof to keep off the rain and the damp night air, you need very little else to enjoy the greatest comfort in the world. Or the delights of paradise.

Anyone who has been following this story with due attention will have found it odd that, after the amusing episode in which solomon kicked the village priest, there has been no further reference to other encounters with the local inhabitants, as if we were crossing a desert rather than a civilised european country, a country, moreover, as even schoolchildren know, that gave new worlds to the world. There were some encounters, but only in passing, in the most literal sense of the phrase, in that people came out of their houses to see who was coming and found themselves face to face with the elephant, and while some crossed themselves in amazement and fear, others, though equally afraid, burst out laughing, probably at the sight of the elephant's trunk. This, however, is nothing in comparison with the enthusiasm and the sheer number of boys and the occasional idle adult who came running from the town of castelo rodrigo when they heard the news about the elephant's journey, although no one knows quite how it got there, the news, that is, not the elephant, who will take some time yet to hove into view. Nervous and excited, the commanding officer gave orders to the sergeant to send someone to ask one of the older boys if the spanish soldiers had arrived. The boy was obviously a galician because he replied with another question, Why are they coming here, is there going to be a war, Answer the question, have the spaniards arrived or not, No, sir, they haven't. The information was passed to the commanding officer, on whose face there immediately appeared the most beatific of smiles. There was no doubt about it, fate seemed determined to favour the portuguese troops.

It took nearly an hour for the whole convoy to enter the town, a caravan of men and beasts so tired that they could barely stand, and with scarcely enough strength to raise an arm or twitch an ear in acknowledgement of the applause with which the inhabitants of castelo rodrigo greeted them. A representative of the mayor guided them to the castle's parade ground, which could easily have accommodated at least ten such convoys. Three members of the castellan's family were waiting there, and they then accompanied the commanding officer on an inspection of the areas available to provide shelter for the men, not forgetting any shelter that the spaniards might need should they decide not to camp outside the castle. The mayor, whom the commanding officer went to see afterwards in order to pay his respects, said, They'll probably pitch camp outside the castle walls, which, apart from anything else, would have the advantage of reducing any possibility of a confrontation, What makes you think there might be a confrontation, asked the commanding officer, You never can tell with spaniards, they've been very cocky since they've had an emperor, and it will be even worse if, instead of the spaniards, the austrians appear, Are they bad people, asked the commanding officer, They think they're superior to everyone else, That's a common enough sin, I, for example, judge myself to be superior to my soldiers, and my soldiers judge themselves to be superior to the porters who came with us to do the heavy work, And the elephant, asked the mayor, smiling, The elephant doesn't have an opinion, he's not of this world, replied the commanding officer, Yes, I watched from a window to see him arrive, and he really is a superb creature, might I have a closer look, He's all yours, Why, I wouldn't know what to do with him, apart from feed him, Well, I should warn you, sir, that he gets through a lot of food, So I've heard, and I certainly have no ambitions to own an elephant, I'm just a town mayor, after all, That is to say neither a king nor an archduke, Precisely, neither a king nor an archduke, I have only what I can call my own. The commanding officer got to his feet, I won't take up any more of your time, sir, thank you very much for your kind welcome, In welcoming you, captain, I was merely serving the king, however, if you would accept my invitation to be a guest in my house for as long as you stay in castelo rodrigo, that would be another matter, Thank you for an invitation that does me far more honour than you can imagine, but I must stay with my men, Yes, I understand, indeed, I have no option but to understand, but I hope you will at least come to supper one day soon, With great pleasure, although that depends on how long I have to wait, what if the spaniards turn up tomorrow, for example, or even today, My scouts outside the walls will give us due warning, How will they do that, With carrier pigeons. The commanding officer gave him a sceptical look, Carrier pigeons, he asked, I've heard of them, but frankly, I can't believe that a pigeon can fly for as many hours as people say, covering enormous distances, only to end up unerringly in the pigeon-house it was born in, You will have the opportunity to see this phenomenon with your own eyes, for with your permission, I will send for you when the pigeon arrives so that you can witness for yourself the removal and reading of the message tied to the bird's leg, If it's true, it won't be long before messages can fly through the air with no need of a pigeon, That would be rather more difficult, I imagine, said the mayor, smiling, but as long as there's a world, anything's possible, As long as there's a world, That's the only way, captain, the world is essential, Look, I mustn't take up any more of your time, It's been a great pleasure talking to you, For me too, sir, indeed, after this long journey, it's been like a glass of cool water, A glass of water that I failed to offer you, Next time perhaps, Don't forget my invitation, said the mayor as the captain was going down the stone steps, I'll be there, sir.

As soon as he entered the castle, the commanding officer summoned the sergeant, to whom he gave orders regarding the immediate fate of the thirty porters. Since they would no longer be needed, they would rest the next day, but go back to lisbon the day after, Tell the quartermaster to prepare a reasonable amount of food for them, thirty men means thirty mouths, thirty tongues and an enormous number of teeth, obviously it won't be possible to provide them with enough food for the entire journey back to lisbon, but they can sort themselves out en route, working or, Or stealing, said the sergeant to fill in the pause, Let's just say they can make do as best they can, said the commanding officer, resorting, for lack of anything better, to one of those phrases that form part of the universal panacea, the perfect example of which is that most barefaced expression of personal and social hypocrisy, namely, urging patience on the poor person to whom one has just refused alms. Those who had taken on the role of foreman wanted to know when they would be paid for their work, and the commanding officer sent word that he did not know, but that they should present themselves at the palace and ask to speak to the secretary or his representative, But I advise you, and the sergeant repeated this advice word for word, not to go there as a group, because that might give entirely the wrong impression, thirty ragamuffins standing outside the palace gate as if about to launch an attack, in my view, only the foremen should go and, when they do, they should make every effort to look as clean and tidy as possible. Later on, one of these men, happening to meet the commanding officer, asked permission to speak and said how much he regretted not being able to continue on to valladolid. The commanding officer didn't know what to say, and for a few seconds, the two men looked at each other in silence, then went about their business.

The commanding officer gave his soldiers a rapid summary of the situation, they would wait for the spanish to arrive, although it wasn't yet known when this would be, there having been no news on that point so far, and he refrained at the last moment from making any reference to carrier-pigeons, aware of the dangers of any relaxation of discipline. He was unaware that among his subordinates were two pigeon-fanciers, a term that did not exist at the time, except perhaps among initiates, but which was doubtless going around knocking at doors, with the absent-minded air affected by all new words, asking to be let in. The soldiers were standing at ease, a position they assumed ad libitum, without making any attempt at elegance. The time will come when standing formally at ease will cost a soldier as much effort as standing to attention does the guards, with the enemy lying in wait on the other side of the street. Bales of hay had been strewn about the floor, thick enough to cushion the soldiers' shoulder blades against the intractable hardness of the flagstones. The muskets were arranged in stacks along one wall. Let's just hope they don't have to use them, thought the commanding officer, concerned that the act of handing over solomon might, through a lack of tact on one side or the other, become instead a casus belli. He clearly remembered the words of the secretary pêro de alcáçova carneiro, not just those in the letter, of course, but the unwritten words he could read between the lines, namely, that if the spanish, or the austrians, or both, behaved in an unpleasant or provocative manner, he should proceed accordingly. The commanding officer could not imagine why the soldiers marching towards them, be they spanish or austrian, would behave provocatively or indeed unpleasantly. A cavalry captain lacks both the intelligence and the political nous of a secretary of state, and he would therefore be wise to allow himself to be guided by someone who knows more than he does, until the moment for action arrived, if it did. The commanding officer was pondering these thoughts when subhro came into the improvised bedroom for which the sergeant had thoughtfully reserved a few bales of hay. When he saw subhro, the commanding officer felt an awkwardness that could only be attributed to an uneasy awareness that he had not yet enquired about solomon's state of health, had not even been to see him, as if once they had reached castelo rodrigo, his mission would be at an end. How's solomon, he asked, When I left him, he was sleeping, replied the mahout, He's a valiant creature, exclaimed the commanding officer with feigned enthusiasm, He just went where he was led, and he was born with whatever strength and resistance he has, they're not personal virtues, You're being very hard on poor solomon, Perhaps because of a story that one of my assistants just told me, What story is that, asked the commanding officer, The story of a cow, Do cows have stories, asked the commanding officer, smiling, This one did, she spent twelve days and twelve nights in the galician mountains, in the cold, rain, ice and mud, among stones as keen as knives and scrub as sharp as nails, enjoying only brief intervals of rest in between fighting and fending off attacks, amid howls and mooing, the story of a cow who was lost in the fields with her calf and found herself surrounded by wolves for twelve days and twelve nights, and was obliged to defend herself and her calf during a long-drawn-out battle, enduring the agony of living on the very edge of death, encircled by teeth and gaping jaws, prone to sudden assaults, knowing that every thrust with her horns had to hit home, as she fought for her own life and for that of the little creature who could not yet fend for itself, and dreading those moments when the calf sought its mother's teats and slowly suckled, while the wolves closed in, crouching low, ears pricked. Subhro took a deep breath, then went on, At the end of those twelve days, the cow and her calf were found and saved and led in triumph to the village, but the story doesn't end there, it went on for two more days, at the end of which, because the cow had turned wild and learned to defend herself, and because no one could tame her or even get near her, she was killed, slaughtered, not by the wolves she had kept at bay for twelve whole days, but by the very men who had saved her, possibly by her actual owner, incapable of understanding that a previously docile, biddable creature, having learned how to fight, could never stop fighting.

A respectful silence reigned for a few seconds in the large stone room. The soldiers present were not very experienced in war, indeed the youngest of them had never even smelled gunpowder on a battlefield, and thus they were astonished at the courage shown by an irrational creature, a cow, imagine that, who had revealed herself to have such human sentiments as love of family, the gift of personal sacrifice, and self-denial carried to the ultimate extreme. The first to speak was the soldier who appeared to know a lot about wolves, That's a very nice story, he said to subhro, and that cow deserved, at the very least, a medal for bravery and merit, but there are a few things about your account that remain unclear and don't quite ring true, For example, asked the mahout in the tone of someone squaring up for a fight, For example, who told you the story, A galician, And where did he hear it, He must have heard it from someone else, Or read it, As far as I know he can't read, All right, perhaps he heard it and memorised it, Possibly, but I was simply interested in re-telling it as best I could, You have an excellent memory, and the language in which you told the story was far from ordinary, Thank you, said subhro, but now I would like to know which bits of the story remain unclear to you and failed to ring true, The first is that we are given to understand or, rather, it is explicitly stated that the struggle between the cow and the wolves lasted twelve days and twelve nights, which would mean that the wolves attacked the cow on the very first night and only withdrew on the twelfth, presumably having sustained some losses, We weren't there to see what happened, No, but anyone who knows anything about wolves would know that, although they live in a pack, they hunt alone, What are you getting at, asked subhro, I'm saying that the cow wouldn't have been able to withstand a concerted attack by three or four wolves for one hour, let alone twelve days, So the whole story of the battling cow is a lie, No, the lie consists only in the exaggerations, linguistic affectations and half-truths that try to pass themselves off as whole truths, So what do you think happened, asked subhro, Well, I think the cow really did get lost, was attacked by a wolf, fought him off and forced him to flee, possibly badly injured, and then stayed where she was, grazing and suckling her calf until she was found, Couldn't another wolf have come along, Yes, but that would be unlikely, and having fought off one wolf is more than enough to justify a medal for bravery and merit. The audience applauded, thinking that, all things considered, the galician cow deserved the truth as much as she deserved the medal.

Gathered together early the next morning, the general assembly of porters made a unanimous decision to take an easier and less perilous route back to lisbon, following friendlier paths that were softer underfoot and where they need not fear the yellow gaze of wolves and the sinuous, roundabout way in which those creatures gradually corral the minds of their victims. Not that wolves are never to be seen in coastal regions, on the contrary, they often are and in large numbers, and make regular raids on flocks of sheep, but there is an enormous difference between walking among craggy outcrops of rock, the mere sight of which makes the heart tremble, and treading the cool sand of beaches frequented by fisherfolk, kindly people always willing to give you half a dozen sardines in exchange for a little help, however symbolic, when hauling in a boat. The porters already have their provisions and are waiting for subhro and the elephant to come and say goodbye. This was probably the mahout's idea, but since there is nothing written on the subject, no one knows quite how it arose. Now one can see how a person could be embraced by an elephant, but the corrresponding gesture is simply unimaginable. And as for shaking hands, that would be impossible, five insignificant human fingers could never grasp one huge great foot the size of a tree-trunk. Subhro had ordered the men to form two lines, five in front and five behind, leaving a distance of about one ell between every two men, which indicated that the elephant was going to do no more than walk past them as if reviewing the troops. Subhro then spoke again to explain that solomon would stop in front of each of them and that they should then hold out

86

their right hand, palm uppermost, and wait for solomon to say goodbye. And don't be afraid, solomon is sad, but he's not angry, he'd grown used to you and has only just found out that you're leaving, How did he find out, That's one of those questions not even worth asking, if you were to ask him directly, he probably wouldn't answer, Is that because he wouldn't know or because he doesn't want to, In solomon's mind, not wanting and not knowing form part of a much larger question about the world in which he finds himself, it's probably the same question we all need to ask, both elephants and men. Subhro immediately felt that he had just said something stupid, a remark that deserved a place of honour on the list of platitudes, Fortunately, he murmured, as he walked off to fetch the elephant, no one had under-stood, that's one good thing about ignorance, it protects us from false knowledge. The men were growing impatient, they couldn't wait to set off, and for safety's sake, they have decided to follow the left bank of the douro river as far as oporto, which had a reputation for offering people a warm welcome and where some of the men had already considered setting up home, once the problem of their wages had been resolved, and that could only be done in lisbon. Each man was thus immersed in his own thoughts when solomon appeared, lumbering along on his four tons of flesh and bones and his three metres of height. Some of the less daring among the men felt a sudden tightening in the stomach when they thought about what could go wrong at this farewell parade, for this is a topic, that of different animal species saying goodbye to one another, on which there is no bibliography. Accompanied by his assistants, whose state of dolce far niente since they left lisbon will soon come to an end, subhro arrived seated on solomon's broad shoulders, and this only served to increase the unease of the men waiting in their lines. The question in every mind was, How can he possibly say goodbye to us when he's so high up. The two lines kept wavering as if shaken by a strong wind, but the porters stood firm and did not scatter. Besides, there would have been no point, the elephant was nearly upon them. Subhro made him stop in front of the man at the extreme right of the first line and said clearly, Hold out your hand, palm uppermost. The man did as ordered, there was his hand, apparently steady. Then the elephant placed the end of his trunk on the open palm, and the man responded instinctively, squeezing the proffered trunk as if it were someone's hand, at the same time trying to suppress the lump forming in his throat, which would, if left unchecked, end in tears. He was shaking from head to toe, while subhro, up above, gazed sweetly down upon him. More or less the same thing happened with the next man, but there were also cases of mutual rejection, where the man preferred not to offer his hand and the elephant withheld his trunk, a kind of powerful, instinctive antipathy that no one could explain, since during the journey nothing had passed between the two that could have presaged such hostility. On the other hand, there were moments of intense emotion, as was the case with one man who burst into heartfelt sobs as if he had been reunited with a loved one from whom he'd been parted for years. The elephant treated him with particular indulgence. He touched the man's head and shoulders with his trunk, bestowing on him caresses that seemed almost human, such was the gentleness and tenderness implicit in every movement. For the first time in the history of humanity, an animal was bidding farewell, in the literal sense, to a few human beings, as if he owed them friendship and respect, an idea unconfirmed by the moral precepts in our codes of conduct, but which can perhaps be found inscribed in letters of gold in the fundamental laws of the elephantine race. A comparative reading of these two documents would doubtless prove most enlightening and would perhaps help us understand the mutually negative reaction that, much to our regret, but for the sake of truth, we were obliged to describe above. Perhaps elephants and men will never really understand each other. Solomon has just trumpeted so loudly that he must have been heard for a whole league around figueira de castelo rodrigo, not a modern league, but one of the older, shorter ones. It's not easy for people like us, who know so little of elephants, to decipher the motives and intentions behind this strident call erupting from solomon's lungs. And if we were to ask subhro what he, in his capacity as expert, thinks about the matter, he would doubtless prefer not to commit himself and would give us instead one of those evasive answers that close the door to any further questions. Despite these uncertainties, inevitable when people are speaking different languages, we feel justified in saying that solomon the elephant enjoyed the farewell ceremony. The porters had already set off. The experience of living alongside soldiers had, almost without their realising it, led them to take on certain habits of discipline such as those that can result from learning how to form into ranks, choosing, for example, between making a column two or three men deep, because these choices make a difference when organising thirty men, the first method would give a column of fifteen rows, a ridiculously long line that could easily break up at the slightest upset, whether individual or collective, whereas the second method would provide a solid block of ten rows, to which you would only have to add shields for it to resemble the roman tortoise formation. The difference is, above all, psychological. Remember, these men have a long march ahead of them and, as is only natural, they will talk to each other, as they go, in order to pass the time. Now, if two men have to walk along together for two or three hours at a time, even if they feel a really strong desire to communicate, they will inevitably, sooner or later, fall into awkward silences and possibly end up loathing each other. One of these men might be unable to resist the temptation to hurl his companion down a steep river bank. People are quite right when they say that three is god's number, the number of peace and concord. When there are three in a group, one of the three can remain silent for a few minutes without that silence being noticed. Trouble could arise, however, if one of the three men has been walking along plotting how best to get rid of his neighbour in order to make off with his share of the provisions, and then invites the third man in the group to collaborate in this reprehensible scheme, only to be met with the regretful answer, I can't, I'm afraid, I've already agreed to help him kill you.

The sound of galloping hooves was heard. It was the commanding officer who had come to say goodbye to the porters and wish them a safe journey, a courtesy one would not expect from an army officer, however good a man he's known to be, and a courtesy that would not be viewed favourably by his superiors, staunch defenders of a precept as old as the cathedral in braga, and which states that there is a place for everything and everything in its place. As a basic principle for running an efficient home, nothing could be more praiseworthy, but it proves to be a bad principle if used to try and tidy people neatly away in drawers. It is clear that the porters, if the murder plots hatching in some of their heads ever come to anything, do not deserve such courteous treatment. Let us then leave them to their fate and turn our attention to this man hurrying towards us as fast as his aged legs will carry him. His breathless words, when he was finally within range, were these, The mayor says to tell you that the pigeon has arrived. So, it was true, carrier-pigeons really could find their way home. The mayor's house was not far from there, but the commanding officer rode his horse as hard as if he were hoping to reach valladolid by lunchtime. Less than five minutes later, he was dismounting at the door to the mansion, running up the stairs and asking the first servant he encountered to take him to the mayor. There was no need, however, for the mayor was already hurrying to greet him, with a look of satisfaction on his face such as only appears, one imagines, on the faces of pigeon-fanciers proud of their protégés' achievements. He's here, he's here, come with me, he cried eagerly. They went out onto a broad, covered balcony in which a huge wicker cage took up most of the wall to which it was affixed. There's our hero, said the mayor. The pigeon still had the message tied to one leg, as its owner was quick to point out, Normally, I remove the message as soon as the bird arrives so that the pigeon won't think he's wasted his time, but in this instance, I wanted to wait so that you could see for yourself, Thank you very much, sir, this is a big day for me, too, you know, Oh, I don't doubt it, captain, there's more to life than halberds and muskets. The mayor opened the door of the cage, reached in and grabbed the pigeon, who put up no resistance and made no attempt to escape, as if he had been wondering why they had been ignoring him all this time. With quick, deft movements the mayor untied the knots, unrolled the message, which was written on a narrow strip of paper that had doubtless been cut to just that size so as not to hamper the bird in any way.

In brief sentences, the scout reported that the soldiers were cuirassiers, about forty of them, all austrians, as was their captain, and as far as he could see, they were not accompanied by any civilians. They're travelling light, remarked the portuguese captain, So it would seem, said the mayor, What about weapons, There's no mention of weapons, presumably because he thought it imprudent to include such information, on the other hand, he says that, at the rate they're travelling, they should reach the frontier tomorrow, at around midday, Early, Perhaps we should invite them to lunch, Forty austrians, sir, I don't think so, however lightly they're travelling, they'll have their own food with them or money to buy it with, besides, they probably won't like the food we eat, anyway, feeding forty mouths isn't something you can do at a moment's notice, and we're already beginning to run short, no, in my view, sir, it would be best if each side took care of itself, and let god take care of us all, Be that as it may, I won't let you off supper tomorrow, Oh, you can count on me, but unless I'm very much mistaken, you're thinking of inviting the austrian captain too, Well spotted, And why, if I may be so bold, are you inviting him, As a politic and placatory gesture, Do you really think such a gesture is necessary, asked the commanding officer, Experience has taught me that when you have two detachments of troops facing each other across a border, anything can happen, Well, I'll do what I can to avoid the worst, because I don't want to lose any of my men, but if I have to use force, I won't hesitate, and now, sir, if you'll permit me, my men are going to have a lot to do, trying to clean up their uniforms to start with, after all, they've been wearing them, come rain or shine, for nearly two weeks now, and having slept in them and got up in them, we look more like an advance party of beggars than a detachment of soldiers,

Of course, captain, tomorrow, when the austrians arrive, I'll be with you, as is my duty, Thank you, sir, if you need me before then, you know where to find me.

Back at the castle, the commanding officer mustered the troops. He did not give a long speech, but in it he said everything that needed to be said. Firstly, that under no circumstances were the austrians to be allowed into the castle, even if they, the portuguese, had to resort to violence to keep them out. That would be war, he went on, and I hope we don't have to go that far, but the more quickly we can convince the austrians that we mean business, the more quickly we will achieve our aims. We will await their arrival outside the castle walls, and we won't move from there even if they attempt to force their way in. As your commanding officer, I will do all the talking, and initially I require just one thing of you, I want each man's face to be like a book open at the page on which these words are written, No entry. If we succeed, and whatever it takes, we must succeed, the austrians will be obliged to camp outside the walls, which will place them, right from the start, in a position of inferiority. It may be that things will not go as smoothly as my words seem to promise, but I guarantee that I will do all I can to say nothing to the austrians that might offend against the honour of the cavalry unit to which we have devoted our lives. Even if there is no fighting, even if not a single shot is fired, victory will be ours, as it will be if they force us to use weapons. These austrians have, in principle, come to figueira de castelo rodrigo solely to welcome us and accompany us to valladolid, but we have reason to suspect that their real aim is to take solomon with them and leave us here looking like fools. If they think that, though, they have another think coming. Tomorrow, by ten o'clock, I want two look-outs posted on the tallest of the castle's towers, just in case the austrians have simply put it about that they'll be arriving at midday in order to catch us out still watering our horses. You never can tell with austrians, added the commanding officer, forgetting that these would be the first and probably the only austrians he would ever meet.

The commanding officer's suspicions proved correct, for shortly after ten o'clock, cries of alarm issued from the look-outs on the towers, Enemy in sight, enemy in sight. While it's true that the austrians, at least in their military version, do not enjoy a good reputation among these portuguese soldiers, the look-outs, by bluntly calling them enemies, are taking a step that common sense cannot but reprove most severely, pointing out to the rash fellows the dangers of making hasty judgements and condemning people without proof. There is, however, an explanation. The look-outs were under orders to give the alarm, but no one, not even the usually prudent commanding officer, had thought to tell them what form that alarm should take. Faced by the dilemma of having to choose between Enemy in sight, which any civilian could understand, and a very unmartial Our visitors are arriving, the uniform they were wearing made the decision for them, and they expressed themselves using the appropriate vocabulary. Even as the last echo of that alert was still ringing in the air, the soldiers had gathered on the battlements to see the enemy, who, at that distance, four or five kilometres away, were nothing but a dark smudge that barely seemed to move and in which, against expectations, one could not even see the glint of their breastplates. A soldier gave an explanation, That's because they've got the sun at their backs, which, we must say, is a much nicer, far more literary way of saying, The light's behind them. The horses, all of them chestnuts or sorrels of varying shades of brown, hence the dark smudge, were advancing at a smart trot. They could even have approached at a walking pace and the difference would have been minimal, but then they would have lost the psychological effect of an apparently unstoppable advance, which, at the same time, gives the impression that everything is completely under control. Obviously a good gallop with swords held high, in charge-of-the-light-brigade mode, would provide their audience with far more spectacular special effects, but it would be absurd to tire the horses more than was strictly necessary for what promised to be such an easy victory. So thought the austrian captain, a man with long experience on the battlefields of central europe, and that is what he told his troops. Meanwhile, castelo rodrigo was preparing itself for combat. The soldiers, having saddled up their horses, led them outside and left them there, guarded by half a dozen of their comrades, those most fitted for a mission, which, had there been any suitable pasture at the door of the castle, would seem to have simply been a matter of letting the animals graze. The sergeant had gone to tell the mayor that the austrians were coming, They'll be a while yet, but we have to be prepared, he said, Fine, said the mayor, I'll go with you. When they reached the castle, the troops were already formed up at the entrance, blocking all access, and the commanding officer was preparing to give his final speech. Attracted by this free equestrian display and by the possibility that the elephant might be brought out, a large part of the town's population, men and women, young and old, had gathered on the parade ground, which led the commanding officer to say quietly to the mayor, With all these people watching, it's unlikely there'll be any hostilities, My thoughts exactly, but you never can tell with austrians, Have you had some bad experiences with them, asked the commanding officer, Neither good nor bad, none in fact, but I know the austrians are always there and that, for me, is enough. The commanding officer nodded in agreement, but had not, in fact, understood the mayor's cryptic remark, unless you took austrian as a synonym for adversary or enemy. For this reason, he decided to move on at once to the speech with which he hoped to raise the possibly flagging spirits of some of the men. Soldiers, he said, the austrian troops are near. They will come and demand to take the elephant to valladolid, but we will not grant their request, even if they try to impose their wishes on us by force. Portuguese soldiers obey only orders issued by their king, by their military and civil superiors and no one else. The king's promise to make a gift of the elephant solomon to his highness the archduke of austria will be kept to the letter, but the austrians must show due respect for the way in which that is done. When we return home, with heads held high, we can be sure that this day will be remembered for ever, and that as long as there is a portugal, it will be said of each man here today, He was at figueira de castelo rodrigo. There wasn't time for this speech to reach its natural conclusion, the point when eloquence runs out of steam and peters out into still worse commonplaces, because the austrians had already reached the parade ground, with, at their head, their commanding officer. There was a smattering of rather lukewarm applause from the assembled crowd. With the mayor at his side, the captain of the lusitanian hosts rode forward the few metres necessary to make it clear that he was receiving the visitors in accordance with the most refined rules of etiquette. It was then that a particular manoeuvre by the austrian soldiers caused their polished steel breastplates to glitter in the sun. This made a great impression on the waiting crowds. Given the applause and the exclamations of surprise coming from all sides, it was clear that the austrian empire had won the initial skirmish without firing a single shot. The portuguese commanding officer realised that he must counter-attack at once, but couldn't see how. He was saved from this predicament by the mayor saying in a whisper, As mayor, I should be the first to speak, keep calm. The commanding officer made his horse step back a little, conscious of the vast difference in power and beauty between his mount and the sorrel mare ridden by the austrian captain. The mayor had already begun to speak, In the name of the population of figueira de castelo rodrigo, whose mayor I am proud to be, I welcome our brave austrian visitors and wish them the greatest success in carrying out the mission that has brought them here, convinced as I am that they will contribute to strengthening the ties of friendship that bind our two countries, so, once more, welcome to figueira de castelo rodrigo. A man mounted on a mule rode forwards and whispered in the ear of the austrian captain, who impatiently averted his face. The man was the translator, the interpreter. When he had finished translating, the captain spoke in a resonant voice, a voice unaccustomed to being listened to by inattentive ears, far less disobeyed, You know why we're here, you know that we have come to fetch the elephant and take him with us to valladolid, it is vital then that we lose no time and begin immediate preparations for the transfer, so that we can leave tomorrow as early as possible, those are the instructions I was given by the person best fitted to issue them, and I will carry out those orders with the authority invested in me. This was clearly no invitation to the waltz. The mayor muttered, That puts paid to supper then, So it would seem, said the commanding officer. Then he, in turn, spoke, The instructions I received, likewise from the person best fitted to issue them, are rather different, but quite simple, namely to accompany the elephant to valladolid and hand him over to the archduke personally, with no intermediaries. From these deliberately provocative words onwards, words that may have serious consequences, we will omit the interpreter's alternating versions, not just in order to expedite the verbal jousting, but to introduce, with some skill, the preliminary idea that the ensuing duel of arguments is being understood by both parties in real time. Here is the austrian captain, I fear that your somewhat narrow attitude will impede a peaceful solution to this dispute, at the centre of which, of course, is the elephant, who, regardless of who takes him, still has to travel to valladolid, there are, though, certain important details to take into consideration, the first of which is the fact that the archduke maximilian, in declaring that he would accept the present, became, ipso facto, the elephant's owner, which means that his highness the archduke's ideas on the matter should prevail over all others, however deserving of respect those may be, I insist, therefore, that the elephant be handed over to me at once, without further delay, otherwise my soldiers will have no option but to enter the castle by force and seize the animal, That's certainly something I'd like to see, but I have thirty men covering the entrance to the castle and I have no intention of telling them to step aside or to make way for your forty men to pass. By now, the parade ground had almost emptied of townspeople, and a smell of burning had begun to fill the air, in cases such as this, there is always the possibility of being hit by a stray bullet or of receiving a blind, slashing blow to the back with a sword, for as long as war is just a spectacle, that's fine, the trouble starts when they want to involve us as players, especially when we lack any preparation or experience. For this reason, few of them heard the austrian captain's response to the portuguese captain's insolence, At a simple order from me and in less time than it takes me to give it, the cuirassiers under my command could sweep away this feeble military force, more symbolic than real, set up to oppose them, and they will do precisely that unless you, as commanding officer, abandon this show of foolish obstinacy, and I feel obliged to warn you that the inevitable human losses, which, on the portuguese side, depending on the degree of their resistance, could well be total, will be your sole and entire responsibility, so don't come to me afterwards with complaints, Since, if I have understood you rightly, you propose killing us all, I hardly see how we could complain, but I imagine that you would have some difficulty in justifying such violence committed against soldiers who are merely defending the right of their king to lay down the rules for the handing over of an elephant offered as a gift to the archduke maximilian of austria, who, in this case, seems to me to have been very poorly advised, both politically and militarily. The austrian captain did not respond at once, the idea that he would have to justify an action with such drastic consequences to both vienna and lisbon was still going round in his head, and each time it went round, the more complicated the matter seemed. Finally, he felt that he had reached a conciliatory proposal, that he and his men should be allowed into the castle so that they could ascertain the elephant's state of health. Your soldiers are not, I assume, horse doctors, replied the Portuguese commanding officer, although as for yourself, I can't be sure, but I rather think that you are not an expert in animal husbandry, therefore I see no point in allowing you to enter, at least not until you have recognised my right to go to valladolid and deliver the elephant personally to his highness the archduke of austria. Another silence from the austrian captain. When no response came, the mayor said, Let me speak to him. After a few minutes, he returned, looking pleased, He agrees, Tell him, said the portuguese captain, that it would be an honour for me to accompany him on that visit. While the mayor was coming and going, the portuguese captain told the sergeant to instruct the troops to form up into two ranks. Once this had been done, he rode forwards until he was side by side with the austrian captain's mare, and he then asked the interpreter to translate his words, Once again, welcome to castelo rodrigo, and now let us go and see the elephant.

Apart from a minor scuffle among some soldiers, three from either side, the journey to valladolid passed off pretty much without incident. In a gesture of good will, worthy of mention, the portuguese captain left the organisation of the convoy, that is, the decision as to who should go in front and who behind, to the austrian captain, who was very clear about his choice, We'll go in front, the others can sort themselves out as they think best or, if they're happy with how things were when they left lisbon, they can stick to that. There were two excellent and obvious reasons why the austrians chose to go in front, the first was the fact that they were, to all intents and purposes, on home territory, and the second, albeit unconfessed, was that, as long as the sky was clear, as it was now, and until the sun reached its zenith, that is, during the mornings, they would have the sun-king straight ahead of them, with obvious benefits for their glittering breastplates. As for recreating the column of men as it was before, we know that this will not be possible, given that the porters are already on their way to lisbon, passing through the place that will, in a still distant future, be the unconquered and ever loyal city of oporto. Anyway, there was no need to give the matter much thought. If they keep to the rule that the slowest in the convoy should be the one to set the pace and therefore the speed of their advance, then it is obvious that the oxen should go behind the cuirassiers, who will, naturally, be free to gallop ahead whenever they wish, so that anyone who comes to the road to watch the procession will not risk confusing, as the castilian proverb has it, *churras* and *merinas*, *churras* being the unwashed fleeces and *merinas* the clean ones, and we use this saying because we are currently in castile and know how effective a little touch of local colour can be. Or, put slightly differently, horses are one thing, especially when ridden by cuirassiers clothed in sunlight, and quite another are two pairs of scrawny oxen drawing a cart laden with a water trough and a few bundles of forage for the elephant that follows immediately behind with a man astride its shoulders. After the elephant comes the detachment of portuguese cavalry, still trembling with pride at their valiant stance on the previous day, when they blocked with their own bodies the entrance to the castle. None of the soldiers will forget, however long they may live, the moment when, having visited the elephant, the austrian captain gave orders to his sergeant to set up camp outside, in the parade ground, It's only for one night, he said to justify this decision, in the shelter of a few oak trees which, given their age, must have seen many things, but never soldiers sleeping in the damp night air beside a castle that could easily have accommodated three whole infantry divisions and their respective military bands. This absolute triumph over the arrogant pretensions of the austrians was also, unusually in the circumstances, a triumph for common sense, because, however much blood might have been spilled in castelo rodrigo, any war between portugal and austria would be, not only absurd, but impracticable, unless the two countries were to rent an area of land in France, for example, more or less halfway between the two contenders, so that they could martial their respective armies and organise a battle. Anyway, all's well that ends well.

Subhro is not entirely sure that he can take much solace from that soothing dictum. Seeing him, perched three metres up and dressed in his brightly coloured new suit of clothes, smart enough to wear to visit his godmother, if he had one, and which he's wearing now, not out of any personal vanity, but to honour the country from which he has come, the gawpers who watch him pass imagine a being endowed with extraordinary powers, when the fact is that the poor indian is shaking at the thought of what his immediate future may hold. He thinks that until they reach valladolid, his job is guaranteed and someone will pay him for his time and his work, because although it may seem easy travelling on the back of an elephant, this could only be the view of someone who has never tried, for example, to make solomon turn right when he wants to turn left. Beyond valladolid, though, the waters grow murky. He thought he had good reason to believe that, from the very first day, his mission was to accompany solomon to vienna, this assumption, however, exists in the realm of the implicit, that if an elephant has his own personal mahout, it's only natural that where one goes, the other goes too. But no one has ever actually looked him in the eye and told him so. That he'll travel as far as valladolid, yes, but nothing more. It is, therefore, inevitable that subhro's imagination should lead him to expect the worst of all possible situations, arriving in valladolid and finding another mahout waiting to take up the baton and continue the journey to vienna, where, thereafter, that new mahout will live high on the hog in the court of archduke maximilian. However, contrary to what one might think, accustomed as we are to placing base material interests above genuine spiritual values, it wasn't the food and the drink and the freshly made bed each day that made subhro sigh, but the sudden revelation that he loved the elephant and did not want to be parted from him, this was not, strictly speaking, either sudden or a revelation, more a latent state of mind, but such states of mind are not to be discounted. If another mahout really was waiting in valladolid to take charge, subhro's reasons of the heart would weigh very little in the archduke's impartial scales. It was then that subhro, swaying to the rhythm of the elephant's steps, said out loud, up there where no one could hear him, I need to have a serious talk with you, solomon. Fortunately, there was no one else present, because they would have thought the mahout was mad and that, as a consequence, the safety of the convoy was at serious risk. From that moment on, subhro's dreams took a different direction. As if he and solomon were a pair of star-crossed lovers, to whose love everyone, for some reason, was violently opposed, subhro, in his dreams, fled with the elephant across plains, climbed hills and scaled mountains, skirted lakes, waded rivers and crossed forests, always keeping one step ahead of their pursuers, the cuirassiers, whose swift-galloping horses proved of little advantage, because an elephant, when he wants to, can move at a fair old pace. That night, subhro, who never slept far from solomon, went over to him, taking care not to wake him, and began to whisper in his ear. He poured his words into that ear in an unintelligible murmur, that could have been hindi or bengali or some other tongue known only to them, a language born and raised during their years of solitude, which was still solitude even when interrupted by the shrieks of the petty noblemen from the court at lisbon, or the mocking cries of the populace of the city and environs, or, before that, the sailors' jibes on the long voyage that brought him and solomon to portugal. Since we have no idea what language he was speaking, we cannot reveal what subhro was saying, but knowing, as we do, the uneasy thoughts preoccupying him, it is not impossible to imagine the conversation. Subhro was simply asking for solomon's help, making certain practical suggestions to him as to how he might behave, for example, showing, by all the expressive, even radical, means open to an elephant, how unhappy he was at his enforced separation from his mahout, should that prove to be the case. A sceptic will object that you can't expect much from a conversation like that, given that the elephant not only did not respond to the mahout's plea, but continued to sleep serenely. That person clearly knows nothing about elephants. If you whisper in their ear in hindi or in bengali, especially when they're asleep, they're just like the genie in the lamp, which, as soon as it's out of the bottle, asks, What is your wish, sir. Whatever the facts, we happen to know that nothing untoward will happen in valladolid. Indeed, the following night, subhro, feeling repentant, asked solomon to ignore what he had said, he had been acting out of rank egotism, which was no way to solve matters, If things turn out as I fear they will, I'm the one who will have to take responsibility and try to convince the archduke to allow us to stay together, but whatever happens, don't do anything, all right, nothing. The same sceptic, were he here, would have no option but to set aside his scepticism for a moment and say, A very nice gesture, this mahout is a very decent fellow, and it's quite true that the best lessons always come from simple folk. With his spirit at peace, subhro went back to his straw mattress and, within a matter of moments, was asleep. When he woke the following morning and remembered his decision of the previous night, he could not help but ask himself, What would the archduke want with another mahout when he already has one. And he continued to unravel his own reasoning, I have the captain of the cuirassiers as my witness and guarantor, he saw us in the castle and couldn't have failed to think how rare it was to see such a perfect conjunction of man and beast, true, he doesn't know much about elephants, but he knows a lot about horses, and that's something. Everyone recognises that solomon has a good heart, but I wonder if, with another mahout, he would have bade farewell to the porters in the way he did. Not that I taught him to do that, I want to make that quite clear, it just sprang spontaneously from his soul, I myself assumed he would go over to them and would, at most, give a little wave with his trunk or trumpet loudly, do a couple of dance steps and then, so long, goodbye, but, knowing him as I do, I began to get an inkling that he was concocting something in that great head of his, something that would astonish us all. I expect a lot has been written about elephants as a species and much more will be written in the future, but I doubt that any of those authors will have been witness to or even heard of an elephantine prodigy that could compare with what I witnessed in castelo rodrigo, barely believing what my own eyes were seeing.

There is some dissension among the cuirassiers. Some, perhaps the younger, still impetuous and more hot-blooded among them, say that their commanding officer, whatever the cost, should have defended to the last the strategy with which he arrived at castelo rodrigo, namely, gaining the immediate and unconditional surrender of the elephant, even if it proved necessary to use force as a persuasive tool. Anything but his sudden capitulation to the provocative stance adopted by the portuguese captain, who seemed almost eager for a fight, even though he must have known with mathematical certainty that, in any confrontation, he would be defeated. They thought that a mere gesture for effect, such as forty swords being simultaneously unsheathed ready for the attack, would have demolished the apparent intransigence of these grubby portuguese and made the doors of the castle swing open to let in their austrian conquerors. Others, equally bemused by the captain's submissive attitude, felt that his first mistake had been to arrive at the castle and, without more ado, declare, Hand over the elephant, we have no time to lose. Any austrian, born and brought up in central europe, knows that in circumstances such as these, you have to know how to talk and charm, that you should first enquire after the health of the family, make some flattering comment about the excellent condition of the portuguese horses and the imposing majesty of castelo rodrigo's fortifications, and only then, like someone suddenly remembering that he had some other matter to deal with as well, Ah, of course, the elephant. Still other soldiers, more aware of the harsh realities of life, argued that if things had gone as their colleagues had wished, they would now be on the road with the elephant, but with nothing to give him to eat, because it would hardly have made sense for the portuguese to despatch the ox-cart, laden with the bundles of forage and the water trough, while they stayed on at castelo rodrigo for who knows how long, waiting to go home, There's only one explanation, said a rather studious-looking corporal, which is that the captain did not, in fact, have orders from the archduke or whoever to demand that the elephant be handed over immediately, and it was only later, en route or once he had reached castelo rodrigo, that the idea occurred to him, If I could cut the portuguese out of this game of cards, he thought, all the glory would go to me and my men. It would be reasonable to ask how anyone harbouring such thoughts and so totally lacking in sincerity could possibly have been appointed captain of a troop of austrian cuirassiers, because, as even a child could understand, that friendly allusion to the soldiers was a mere tactic to disguise his own, all-excluding ambition. A shame really. We are, more and more, our own defects and not our qualities.

As if in preparation for a major procession, the city of valladolid had decided to put on all its pomp to receive the long-awaited pachyderm, even going so far as to adorn the balconies with draperies and some rather faded bunting that fluttered in the now almost autumnal breeze. Dressed as cleanly as was feasible in those unhygienic times, families filled the not so clean streets, impelled by two principal objectives, finding out where the elephant was and what would happen afterwards. There were a few spoilsports who declared that the elephant was just a rumour, who might possibly appear one day, although there was no telling when that might be. There were others who swore that the poor, exhausted creature had been resting since its arrival yesterday, after the long, hard road it had travelled in order to reach valladolid, first from lisbon to figueira de castelo rodrigo, and then from the portuguese frontier to this city which, for the last two years, has had the honour of being home to those lofty personages, his royal highness the archduke maximilian and his wife, maria, daughter of the emperor charles the fifth, in their roles as regents of spain. We note this only to show the importance of these people, all of them belonging to the most royal of royalties, who lived in the time of solomon and, somehow or another, not only had direct knowledge of his existence, but also of his epic and so far pacific exploits. Right now, the archduke and his wife are watching, entranced, as the elephant is being washed, in the presence of distinguished members of the court and the clergy and a few artists expressly summoned in order to immortalise on paper, wood and canvas the animal's face and his imposing physique. The elephant's alter ego subhro is in charge of operations, which, once again, feature large quantities of water and that same long-handled broom. Subhro is happy because, since he arrived more than twenty-four hours ago, he has seen no sign of a replacement mahout, although he has been told officially by the archduke's steward that, from now on, solomon will be called suleiman. He disliked this change of name intensely, but, as they say, you might lose your rings, but you still have your fingers. Suleiman, let us resign ourselves, we have no option but to call him that, was greatly improved by this general clean-up, but he became truly splendid, dazzling even, when a few servants, after much effort, managed to throw over him a vast saddlecloth on which twenty embroiderers had laboured ceaselessly for weeks, a work whose peer it would be hard to find anywhere in the world, such was the abundance of gems, which, while not all precious stones, glittered as if they were, not to mention the gold thread and the opulent velvets. A ridiculous waste, grumbled the archbishop to himself, from his seat not far from the archduke, instead of squandering money on that beast, they could have embroidered a magnificent canopy for the cathedral, so that we don't always have to process beneath the same old one, as if we were some second-rate village somewhere, not the city of valladolid. A gesture from the regent interrupted these subversive thoughts. There was no need to understand his words, the movements made by the royal hands were enough, pointing first up, then down, it was clear that the archduke wished to speak to the mahout. Accompanied by a minor court dignatory, subhro felt as if he were dreaming a dream he had already dreamt, when, in the filthy enclosure at belém, he was led over to a man with a long beard who turned out to be the king of portugal, joão the third. The gentleman who has just summoned him has no beard, his face is perfectly cleanshaven, and he is, we can say without fear or favour, a fine figure of a man. Beside him sits his beautiful wife, the archduchess maria, the beauty of whose face and body will not last long because she will go on to give birth no less than sixteen times, ten boys and six girls. Monstrous. Subhro is now standing before the archduke, waiting for the questions to begin. As was perfectly foreseeable, the first question was inevitably, What is your name, My name is subhro, sir, Sub what, Subhro, sir, that is my name, And does your name mean anything, It means white, sir, In which language, In bengali, sir, one of the languages of india. The archduke fell silent for a few seconds, and then asked, Are you from india, Yes, sir, I travelled to portugal with the elephant two years ago, Do you like your name, It wasn't my choice, it was the name I was given, sir, Would you choose another if you could, I'm not sure, sir, I've never thought about it, What would you say if I made you change your name, Your highness would need to have a reason, And I do. Subhro did not respond, he knew all too well that one is not allowed to ask questions of kings, that must be why it has always been so difficult, not to say impossible, to get an answer out of any of them regarding the doubts and perplexities besetting their subjects. Then archduke maximilian said, Your name is hard to pronounce, So I have been told, sir, No one in vienna will be able to understand it, That will be my misfortune, sir, But there is a remedy, from now on you will be called fritz, Fritz, said subhro in a pained voice, Yes, it's an easy name to remember, besides there are an enormous number of fritzes in austria already,

112

so you'll be one among many, but the only one with an elephant, If your highness permits, I would prefer to keep my own name, No, I've decided, and I warn you, I'll be angry if you ask again, just get it into your head that your name is fritz and no other, Yes, sir. Then the archduke, rising from his sumptuous seat, said in a loud and sonorous voice, Listen closely, this man has just accepted the name of fritz, which I have bestowed on him, and this fact, as well as the responsibility he bears as keeper of the elephant suleiman, leads me to determine that he be treated by all of you with consideration and respect, and anyone disregarding my wishes will suffer the consequences of my displeasure. This warning was not well received, the momentary murmur that followed was full of all kinds of emotions, disciplined deference, benevolent irony, wounded irritation, imagine, having to behave as respectfully towards a mahout, an animal-tamer, a man who stinks of wild beasts, as if he were a peer of the realm, although one thing is sure, the arch-duke will soon forget this caprice of his. It should be said, for truth's sake, that another murmur quickly followed the first, one devoid of any hostile or contradictory feelings, because it was a murmur of pure admiration, when the elephant lifted the mahout up with the aid of his trunk and one of his tusks and deposited him on his ample shoulders, as spacious as a threshing floor. Then the mahout said, We were subhro and solomon, now we will be fritz and suleiman. He was not speaking to anyone in particular, he was talking to himself, knowing that those names meant nothing, even though they had replaced their original names, which did mean something. I was born to be subhro, not fritz, he thought. He guided suleiman into the enclo-sure assigned to him, a courtyard in the palace, which, despite being an inner courtyard, had easy access to the outside, and there he left him with his food and his water trough, as well as the company of the two assistants who had come with them from lisbon. Subhro, or fritz, it's going to be hard to get used to that change of name, needs to speak to the commanding officer, our commanding officer, for the captain of the austrian cuirassiers has not re-appeared, he must be doing penance for the pathetic figure he cut at figueira de castelo rodrigo. It isn't quite time to say goodbye, for the portuguese don't leave until tomorrow, he simply wants to talk a little about the life that awaits him and to tell the captain that his name and the elephant's have been changed. And to wish the captain and his soldiers a safe journey home and, yes, to say goodbye for ever. The soldiers are camped a little way from the city, in a leafy place with a clear stream running through it, a stream in which most of them have already bathed. The commanding officer went to meet subhro and, seeing the worried look on his face, asked, Has something happened, They've changed our names, I'm fritz now and solomon is suleiman, Who changed them, The only person who could, the arch-duke, But why, He presumably has his reasons, but in my case it was because he found subhro too hard to pronounce, We got used to it, Yes, but he doesn't have anyone to tell him that he ought to get used to it. There was an awkward silence, which the commanding officer broke as best he could, We're leaving tomorrow, he said, Yes, I know, replied subhro, I'll come and say goodbye then, Will we see each other again, asked the commanding officer, Probably not, vienna is a long way from lisbon, That's a shame, now that we're friends, Friend is a big word, sir, and I'm just a mahout who has been ordered to change his name, And I'm just a captain of cavalry who has undergone some inner change during this journey, Was it seeing wolves for the first time, Oh, I saw one years ago, when I was a child, I can't quite remember when, Seeing wolves must change people a lot though, They weren't the reason for the change, The elephant then, That's more likely, although, while I can more or less understand a cat or a dog, I can't understand an elephant, Cats and dogs live side by side with us, and that makes the relationship easier, even if we get things wrong, that continuous intimacy is sure always to resolve any problems, on the other hand, we don't know if they, too, get things wrong and are aware that they do, And the elephant, As I said to you once before, the elephant is a different matter altogether, every elephant contains two elephants, one who learns what he's taught and another who insists on ignoring it all, How do you know, When I realised that I'm just like the elephant, that a part of me learns and the other part ignores everything I've learned, and the longer I live, the more I ignore, Your word games are beyond me, It's not me playing games with words, it's them playing games with me, When does the archduke leave, In three days' time, I believe, Well, I'll miss you, And I'll miss you, said subhro, or fritz. The commanding officer held out his hand to him, and subhro shook it very gently, as if not wanting to hurt him, We'll see each other tomorrow, he said, Yes, we'll see each other tomorrow, repeated the captain. Then they turned their backs on each other and walked away. Neither of them turned round.

Early the following day, subhro returned to the encampment, this time with the elephant. He was accompanied by the two assistants, who had immediately climbed aboard the ox-cart, looking forward to the most pleasant of rides.

The soldiers were awaiting the order to mount. The commanding officer went over to the mahout and said, This is where we go our separate ways, Well, I wish you and your men a good journey, captain, You and solomon still have a long journey ahead of you, it will be winter, I reckon, before you reach vienna, Solomon carries me on his back, so it won't prove too tiring for me, Those lands, I've heard, are very cold, full of snow and ice, things you never had to suffer in lisbon, Although you must admit it could be chilly sometimes, sir, Yes, lisbon is, of course, the coldest city in the world, said the captain, smiling, what saves it from being so is its geographical position. Subhro smiled too, he was enjoying the conversation, they could stay there all morning and afternoon and leave the next day, what difference would it make, I wonder, to arrive home twenty-four hours later. It was then that the commanding officer decided to make his farewell speech, Soldiers, subhro has come to say goodbye to us, and to our great joy, he has brought with him the elephant whose safe-keeping has been our responsibility for the last few weeks. Sharing my time with this man has been one of the happiest experiences of my life, perhaps because india knows things that we do not. I couldn't say with confidence that I know him well, but I can say with absolute certainty that he and I could be, not just friends, but brothers. Vienna is a long way away, lisbon is farther still, and we probably will not see each other again, and perhaps it's better that way, to keep the recollection of these past days so that it can be said of us modest portuguese soldiers that we, too, have the memory of an elephant. The captain spoke for another fifteen or so minutes, but he had said what was most important. While he was speaking, subhro was wondering what solomon would do, if he would behave as he had when he said goodbye to the porters, but repetitions almost always disappoint, the shine goes off them, they noticeably lack spontaneity, and if spontaneity is lacking, so is everything else. It would be best if we simply parted, thought the mahout. The elephant, however, thought otherwise. When the speech had ended, and the captain came over to subhro in order to embrace him, solomon took two steps forward and with the end of his trunk, that vital, feeling lip, he touched the captain's shoulder. The farewell to the porters had been, shall we say, more theatrical, but this, perhaps because the soldiers were used to a different sort of farewell, Do honour to your country, for your country's eyes are upon you, that kind of thing, touched their hearts, and not a few, with some embarrassment, had to wipe away tears with the sleeve of their pea coat or jacket, or whatever they called that item of military clothing then. The mahout accompanied solomon on this inspection, which was also his way of saying goodbye. He was not a man to show his feelings in public, even when, as now, invisible tears are running down his cheeks. The column of men set off, with the ox-cart at the front, and that was that, we will not see them in this theatre again, but such is life, the actors appear, then leave the stage, as is only fitting, it's what usually and always will happen sooner or later, they say their part, then disappear through the door at the back, the one that opens onto the garden. Up ahead, the road curves, the soldiers rein in their horses in order to raise one arm and wave a last goodbye. Subhro does likewise and solomon trumpets in his loudest, most heartfelt way, and that is all they can do, the curtain has fallen and will not rise again.

It was raining on the morning of the third day, which was especially irritating for the archduke, because, although he did not lack for people to organise the convoy in the most useful and efficient way, he had insisted on deciding for himself just where in the cortège the elephant should be. This was a simple matter, suleiman would travel immediately in front of the carriage that would transport the archduke and the archduchess. A trusted confidant begged him to consider the well-known fact that elephants, like horses, for example, defecate and urinate while on the move, Such a spectacle will, inevitably, offend the sensibilities of your highnesses, said the confidant, adopting an expression of the profoundest civic concern, but the archduke told him not to worry, there would always be people in the convoy who could sweep the road whenever these natural depositions occurred. The worst thing was the rain. The rain would affect neither the mood nor the pace of the elephant, indeed, so accustomed was he to the monsoon that, for the last two years, he had missed it greatly, no, the problem requiring a solution was the archduke. It's perfectly understandable really. Crossing half of spain behind an elephant and not being able to use what was, perhaps, the finest embroidered saddlecloth in the world, which he himself had ordered to be made, simply because the rain would leave it so badly damaged that it wouldn't even serve as the canopy for a village church, that, as far as the archduke was concerned, would be the worst disappointment of his entire reign as archduke. Maximilian would not move one step until suleiman was properly covered, with the ornate saddlecloth glinting in the sun. This is what he said, The rain is sure to stop at some point, so let us wait until it does. And so it was. The rain did not stop for two whole hours, but after that, the sky began to clear, there were still a few clouds, but not so dark, and suddenly, it stopped raining, and when the sun finally showed itself, the air, in those first rays, grew lighter, almost transparent. The archduke was so pleased that he allowed himself to give the archduchess' thigh a mischievous squeeze. Then, having recovered his composure, he summoned an aide-de-camp whom he ordered to gallop to the head of the convoy, to where the glittering cuirassiers were waiting, Tell them to set off at once, he said, we have to make up for lost time. Meanwhile, the relevant servants had arrived bearing the vast saddlecloth and, with some difficulty, following fritz's instructions, they spread it over suleiman's powerful back. Then fritz, wearing a suit of clothes, which, in quality of fabric and luxury of cut, far outshone the one he had brought with him from lisbon and which had made such a dent in the treasury's coffers, was lifted onto suleiman's back, from where, to front and rear, he enjoyed an imposing view of the whole convoy. No one was above him, not even the archduke of austria with all his power. The archduke might be able to change the names of a man and an elephant, but with his eyes at the level of the most ordinary of people, he was being carried along inside a carriage where all the perfumes in the world could not quite disguise the foul smells wafting in from without.

You will probably want to know whether this whole convoy will be going to vienna. The answer is no. Most of those travelling here in great state will go no further than the seaport of the town of rosas, near the french border. There they will say farewell to the archduke and archduchess, will doubtless watch the embarkation, and, above all, observe with some trepidation what effect suleiman's four brute tons will have on the ship, if its quarterdeck will withstand such a weight, or if they will have to return to valladolid with the tale of a shipwreck to tell. The gloomier among them foresee the damage that could be caused to the vessel and its safety if the elephant, alarmed by the swaying of the boat, became nervous and unable to keep its footing, I don't even want to think about it, they said woefully to their companions, savouring the possibility of being able to announce later on, I told you so. Ignore those wet blankets, this elephant has come from far away, from distant india, fearlessly facing the storms of the indian ocean and the atlantic, and here he is, steadfast and determined, as if he had never done anything all his life but travel by boat. Now, though, it is a matter of covering distances, long distances. A glance at the map is enough to make you feel tired. And yet it looks as if everything were so close, within easy reach, so to speak. The explanation, of course, lies in the scale. It's easy to accept that a centimetre on the map equals twenty kilometres in reality, but what we tend not to consider is that, in the process, we ourselves suffer an equivalent dimensional reduction, which is why, being but specks on the earth's surface, we are still smaller on maps. It would be interesting to know, for example, how much a human foot would measure on that same scale. Or the foot of an elephant. Or archduke maximilian of austria's entire entourage.

Only two days had passed and already the cortège had lost much of its splendour. The persistent rain that fell on the morning of their departure had dire effects on the draperies of both coaches and carriages, but also on the clothes of those who, in the line of duty, had to brave the elements for longer or shorter periods of time. Now the convoy is travelling through a region where it appears not to have rained since the world began. The dust

begins to rise up at the passing of the cuirassiers, whom
the rain had not spared either, for a breastplate is not a
hermetically sealed box, its component parts do not always
fit perfectly together and the chains connecting them leave
gaps through which swords and spears can easily penetrate,
in the end, all that splendour, proudly displayed in figueira
de castelo rodrigo, is of little practical use. Then comes a
huge line of carts, wagons, coaches and carriages of all types
and for all purposes, whether carrying baggage or transporting squadrons of servants, and they raise still more dust
which, for lack of wind, will hang in the air until close of
day. This time those in charge failed to observe the precept
that the speed of the slowest should determine the speed
of the whole convoy. The two ox-carts laden with the
elephant's food and water were relegated to the rear of the
cortège, which means that every now and then the whole
convoy has to stop so that the laggards can catch up. What
really gets on everyone's nerves, starting with the archduke,
who can barely disguise his irritation, is suleiman's obliga-
tory afternoon nap, a rest that benefits only him, but which,
in the end, they all take advantage of, not that this prevents
them complaining, At this rate we'll never arrive. The first
time that the convoy stopped and word went round that
this was because suleiman had to rest, the archduke
summoned fritz to ask just who did he think was in charge,
well, he didn't put the question quite like that, an archduke
of austria would never stoop so low as to admit that anyone
other than himself could possibly be in charge wherever he
happened to be, but even given the decidedly popular tone
in which we have couched the question, the only appropriate response would have been for fritz, out of shame, to
have prostrated himself on the ground. Over the days,

though, we have had occasion to note that subhro is not a man to be easily cowed, and now, in his new incarnation, it is difficult, if not impossible, to imagine him struck dumb by an attack of timidity, with his tail between his legs, saying, What are your orders, sir. His reply was exemplary, Unless the archduke of austria delegates his authority, absolute power belongs to him by right and tradition, as is acknowledged by his subjects, both natural and, as in my own case, acquired, You speak like a scholar, Oh, I am merely a mahout who has read a little of life's book, What's this business with suleiman, what's all this about him having to rest during the early part of the afternoon, That is the custom in india, sir, We're in spain now, not india, If your highness knew elephants as I believe I do, you would know that india exists wherever an indian elephant happens to be, and I am not speaking here of african elephants, of whom I have no experience, and that same india will, whatever happens, always remain intact inside him, That's all very well, but I have a long journey ahead of me and that elephant is making me lose three or four hours a day, from now on, suleiman will rest for one hour and one hour only, Regretfully, your highness, and believe me, I feel an utter wretch not to be able to agree with you, one hour will not be enough, We'll see. The order was given, but swiftly cancelled the following day. We have to be logical, fritz was saying, just as I would not expect anyone to think it a good idea to reduce by one third the amount of food and water suleiman needs to live, I cannot agree, without protest, to taking away from him the larger part of his deserved rest, without which he could not survive the huge effort demanded of him each day, it's true that an elephant in the indian jungle walks many kilometres from dawn till dusk, but there he is in his own land, not in this bleak place without enough shade to accommodate a cat. Let us not forget that when fritz was called subhro he raised no objection to solomon's rest being reduced from four hours to two, but those were different times, the captain of the portuguese cavalry was a man with whom one could speak, a friend, not an authoritarian archduke, who, aside from being charles the fifth's son-in-law, has no other obvious merits to recommend him. Fritz was being unfair, he should at least have felt obliged to acknowledge that no one had ever treated suleiman as had this now despised archduke of austria. Think only of that saddle-cloth. Not even elephants owned by rajahs in india were spoiled like that. Nevertheless, the archduke was not happy, there was too much rebellion in the air for his liking. Punishing fritz for his dialectical boldness would be more than justified, but the archduke knows perfectly well that he would not find another mahout in vienna. And if, by some miracle, that rara avis should exist, there would have to be an interim period during which he and the elephant got to know each other, otherwise there could be no saying how such a large animal would behave, for as far as any human being was concerned, archdukes included, predicting his mind was like placing an entirely random bet with few prospects of winning. The elephant was, in truth, a completely alien being. So much so that he had nothing whatever to do with this world, he governed himself by rules that would not fit any known moral code, to the point that, as soon became evident, he couldn't care less whether he travelled in front of or behind the archducal coach. The archduke and archduchess could no longer bear the repeated spectacle of suleiman's dejecta, not to mention having to breathe in the fetid odours that these gave off, their delicate nostrils being accustomed to very different aromas. In fact, the archduke wanted to punish fritz not the elephant, who was now relegated to a secondary position after a few days of seeming to everyone present to be one of the grand figures of the entourage. He is still near the head of the convoy, but now he will never see anything but the rear of the archduke's coach. Fritz suspects that he is being punished, but he can't plead for justice because that same justice, in deciding to change the position of the elephant in the convoy, was merely preventing the sensorial discomforts caused to archduke maximilian and his wife maria, daughter of charles the fifth. Having resolved that problem, the other problem was also resolved, and that very night too. Cheered to see the elephant demoted to the status of mere follower, maria asked her husband to relieve suleiman of the saddlecloth, I think that wearing it on his back is a punishment poor suleiman does not deserve, and besides, Besides what, asked the archduke, Once one has got over the shock of seeing such a large, imposing animal clothed in what looks like some kind of ecclesiastical vestment, the sight rapidly becomes ridiculous, grotesque, and the longer one looks at him, the more grotesque he becomes, It was my idea, said the archduke, but I think you're right, I'll have the saddlecloth sent to the bishop of valladolid, I'm sure he'll find some use for it, and I'm sure, too, that if we were to stay in spain, we would have the pleasure of seeing one of the best dressed generals of our holy mother church processing beneath a saddlecloth turned canopy.

There were even those who had predicted that the elephant's journey would end right here, in the sea at rosas, either because the gangway collapsed, unable to bear suleiman's four tons of weight, or because a large wave knocked him off balance and hurled him headfirst into the deep, and thus the once happy solomon, now sadly baptised with the barbarous name of suleiman, would have met his final hour. Most of the noble personages who had come to rosas to bid farewell to the archduke had never in their lives set eyes on an elephant. They do not know that such an animal, especially if, at some point in its life, it has travelled by sea, has what is usually termed good sea legs. Don't ask him to help steer the ship, use the octant or the sextant, or climb the yardarms to reef the sails, but place him at the helm, on the four stout stakes that serve him as legs, and summon up the stiffest of storms. Then you'll see how an elephant can happily face the fiercest of headwinds, close-hauling with all the elegance and skill of a first-class pilot, as if that art were contained in the four books of the vedas that he had learned by heart at a tender age and never forgotten, even when the vicissitudes of life determined that he would earn his sad daily bread carrying tree trunks back and forth or putting up with the loutish curiosity of certain lovers of vulgar circus shows. People have very mistaken ideas about elephants. They imagine that elephants enjoy being forced to balance on a heavy metal ball, on a tiny curved surface on which their feet barely fit. We're just fortunate that they're so good-natured, especially those that come from india. They realise that a lot of patience is required if they are to put up with us human beings, even when we pursue and kill them in order to saw off or extract their tusks for the ivory. Among themselves, elephants often remember the famous words spoken by one of their prophets, Forgive them, lord, for they know not what they do. For 'they' read 'us', especially those who came here to see if suleiman would die and who have now begun the journey back to valladolid, feeling as frustrated as that spectator who used to follow a circus company around wherever it went, simply in order to be there on the day that the acrobat missed the safety-net. Ah, yes, there was something else we meant to say. As well as the elephant's indisputable competence at the helm, over all the centuries in which man has put to sea, no one has yet found anyone to rival an elephant for working the capstan.

Having installed suleiman in a part of the deck surrounded by bars, whose function, despite their apparent robustness, was more symbolic than real, since they were entirely dependent on the animal's frequently erratic moods, fritz went off in search of news. The first and most obvious thing he needed to know was the answer to the question, Where is the boat heading, a question he asked of an old sailor with a kindly face, and from whom he received the prompt, brief and enlightening answer, To genoa, And where's that, asked the mahout. The man seemed to have difficulty understanding how it was possible for anyone anywhere in the world not to know where genoa was, and so he merely pointed eastwards and said, Over there, In italy, then, suggested fritz, whose limited geographical knowledge nevertheless allowed him to take certain risks. Yes, in italy, confirmed the sailor, And vienna, where is that, asked fritz, Much further north, beyond the alps, What are the alps, The alps are huge great mountains, very difficult to cross, especially in winter, not that I've been there myself, but I've heard tell of travellers who have, If that's true, poor solomon is going to have a bad time of it, he comes from india, you see, which is a hot country, he's never experienced real cold, neither of us has, because I'm from india too, Who's solomon, asked the sailor, Solomon was the name the elephant had before he was renamed suleiman, just as I am now fritz even though my name has been subhro ever since I came into the world, Who changed your names, The only person with the power to do so, his highness the archduke, who is travelling on this boat, Is he the elephant's owner, asked the sailor, Yes, and I am his keeper, his carer, or his mahout, which is the correct term, solomon and I spent two years in portugal, which isn't the worst of places to live, and now we're on our way to vienna, which, they say, is the very best, It has that reputation, Well, let's hope it lives up to its reputation and that they finally let poor solomon rest, he wasn't made for all this travelling about, the voyage we had to make from goa to lisbon was quite enough, solomon, you see, originally belonged to the king of portugal, dom joão the third, but when he offered him as a gift to the archduke, it fell to me to accompany solomon, first on the voyage to portugal and now on this long journey to vienna, That's what they call seeing the world, said the sailor, Not as much of it as you would see travelling from port to port, replied the mahout, but he could not complete his sentence because the archduke was approaching, followed by the inevitable entourage, but without the archduchess, who, it would seem, now viewed suleiman rather less sympathetically. Subhro shrank back out of the way, as if thinking that he would thus go unnoticed, however, the archduke spotted him, Fritz, come with me, I'm going to see the elephant, he said. The mahout stepped forward, not knowing quite where to stand, but the archduke clarified matters for him, Go on ahead and see if everything is in order, he said. This proved fortunate because suleiman, in the absence of his mahout, had decided that the wooden deck was the best possible place on which to do his business and, as a consequence, he was literally skating about on a thick carpet of excrement and urine. Beside him, so that he could quench any sudden thirst without delay, was the water trough, still almost full, as well as a few bundles of forage, although only a few, since the others had been taken down into the hold. Subhro thought quickly. With the help of some five or six sailors, all reasonably strong, he managed to tip the water out of the trough so that it poured in a cascade across the deck and straight into the sea. The effect was almost instantaneous. Thanks to that rush of water and its dissolving properties, the stinking soup of excrement was swept overboard, apart from what remained stuck to the soles of the elephant's feet, but a second, less abundant stream left him in a more or less acceptable state, proving, yet again, that not only is the best the enemy of the good, the good, however hard it tries, will never even be fit to tie best's shoelaces. The archduke can now appear. Before he does, though, let us reassure those readers concerned by the lack of information about the ox-cart that had transported the water trough and the bundles of forage the whole one hundred and forty leagues from valladolid to rosas. The french have a saying, which they were just beginning to use around that time, pas de nouvelles, bonnes nouvelles, so our readers can stop worrying, the ox-cart is on its way back to valladolid, where damsels of every social class are weaving garlands of flowers in order to adorn the horns of the oxen when they arrive, and don't ask them precisely why they are doing this, one of them was apparently heard to say, although we don't know to whom, that the crowning of working oxen with a wreath was an ancient custom, dating perhaps from the time of the greeks or romans, and given that walking to rosas and back, a distance of some two hundred and eighty leagues, definitely counted as work, the idea was received with enthusiasm by the community of nobles and plebeians in valladolid, which is now considering putting on a great popular festival with jousting, fireworks, the distribution of food, clothes and alms to the poor and whatever else occurs to the inhabitants' excited imaginations. Now what with all these explanations, indispensable to our readers' present and future peace of mind, we missed the moment when the archduke actually reached the elephant, not that you missed very much, for in the course of this story, the same arch- duke, as we have both described and not described, has arrived many times at various places entirely without inci- dent, as court protocol demands, for if it did not, it would not be protocol. We know that the archduke enquired after the health and well-being of his elephant suleiman and that fritz gave him the appropriate replies, especially those that his archducal highness would most like to hear, which shows just how much the once shabby mahout has learned during his apprenticeship in the delicacies and wiles of the perfect courtier, for the innocent portuguese court, more inclined to the religious hypocrisy of the confessional and the sacristy than to the refinements of the salon, had not served him as a guide, indeed, confined to that rather grubby enclosure in belém, he had never been given the least opportunity to broaden his education. It was noticed that the archduke occasionally wrinkled his nose and made constant use of his perfumed handkerchief, which would, of course, have surprised the cast-iron olfactory systems of the sailors, accustomed to all kinds of pestilential smells and therefore insensitive to the odour that, despite the wind, still lingered in the air after that sluicing down of the decks. Having done his duty as a proprietor concerned for the safety of his possessions, the archduke hurriedly retreated, followed by the usual colourful peacock's tail of court parasites.

Once the loading of the ship was completed, and this required more than usually complex calculations, given that there were four tons of elephant stowed on one small area of the deck, the ship was ready to set sail. Having weighed anchor and hoisted its sails, one square and the others triangular, the latter reclaimed a century or so before from their remote mediterranean past by portuguese sailors, and which, later on, were called lateens, the ship, initially, swayed clumsily on the waves, and then, after the first flap of the sails, headed east, for genoa, just as the sailor had told the mahout. The crossing lasted three long days, with mostly rough seas and gale-force winds that hurled furious squalls of rain down onto the elephant's back and onto the sacking with which the sailors on deck were trying to protect themselves from the worst. There was not a sign of the archduke, who was safe inside in the warm with the archduchess, doubtless keeping in practice in order to produce his third child. When the rain stopped and the wind ran out of puff, the passengers from below decks began to emerge, unsteady and blinking, into the dim light of day, looking very green about the gills and with dark circles under their eyes, and the cuirassiers' attempt, for example, to dredge up an artificially martial air from now distant memories of terra firma, including, if they really had to, the memory of castelo rodrigo, even though they had been most shamefully defeated there by those humble, ill-mounted, ill-equipped portuguese horsemen, and without a single shot being fired. When the fourth day dawned, with a calm sea and a clear sky, the horizon had become the coast of liguria. The beam sent out from the genoa lighthouse, a landmark known affectionately by the locals as the lantern, faded as the morning brightness grew, but it was still strong enough to guide any vessel into port. Two hours later, with a pilot on board, the ship was entering the bay and slipping slowly, with almost all its sails furled, towards a vacant mooring at the quay where, as became immediately patent and manifest, all kinds of carriages and carts of various types and for various purposes, almost all of them harnessed to mules, were awaiting the convoy. Given how slow, laborious and inefficient communications were in those days, one must presume that carrier-pigeons had once again played an active part in the complex logistical operation that made this quayside welcome possible, bang on time, with no delays or setbacks that would have meant one contingent having to wait for the other. We hereby recognise that the somewhat disdainful, ironic tone that has slipped into these pages whenever we have had cause to speak of austria and its people was not only aggressive, but patently unfair. Not that this was our intention, but you know how it is with writing, one word often brings along another in its train simply because they sound good together, even if this means sacrificing respect for levity and ethics for aesthetics, if such solemn concepts are not out of place in a discourse such as this, and often to no one's advantage either. It is in this and other ways, almost without our realising it, that we make so many enemies in life.

The first to appear were the cuirassiers. They led their horses out so that they would not slip on the gangway. The cavalry horses, normally the objects of great care and attention, have a rather neglected air about them, evidence that they need a good brushing to smooth their coats and make their manes gleam. As they appear to us now, one might say that they bring shame upon the austrian cavalry, a most unfair judgement that would seem to have forgotten the long, long journey from valladolid to rosas, seven hundred kilometres of continuous marching, of wild winds and rain, interspersed by the occasional bout of sweltering sun and, above all, dust and more dust. It's hardly surprising, then, that the newly disembarked horses have the rather faded look of second-hand goods. Nevertheless, we can see how, at a short distance from the quay, behind the curtain formed by the carts, carriages and wagons, the soldiers, under the direct command of the captain we have already met, are doing their best to improve the appearance of their mounts, so that the guard of honour for the archduke, when the moment arrives for him to disembark, will be as dignified as one would expect at any event involving the illustrious house of habsburg. Since the archduke and the archduchess will be the last to leave the ship, it is highly likely that the horses will have time to recover at least a little of their usual splendour. At the moment, the baggage is being unloaded, along with the dozens of chests, coffers and trunks containing the clothes and the thousand and one objects and adornments that constitute the noble couple's ever-expanding trousseau. The general public are also here, and in great numbers too. The rumour that the archduke of austria was about to disembark and with him an elephant from india had raced through the city like a lit fuse, and the immediate result was that dozens of men and women, all equally curious, had rushed down to the port, and in no time there were hundreds of them, so many that they were getting in the way of the unloading and loading. They couldn't see the archduke, who had not yet emerged from his cabin, but the elephant was there, standing on the deck, huge and almost black, with that thick trunk as flexible as a whip, with those tusks like pointed sabres, which, in the imagination of the inquisitive, unaware of suleiman's placid temperament, would doubtless be used as powerful weapons of war before being transformed, as they inevitably will be, into the crucifixes and reliquaries that have filled the christian world with objects carved out of ivory. The person gesticulating and giving orders on the quay is the archduke's steward. One rapid glance of his experienced eye is enough to decide which cart or wagon should carry which coffer, chest or trunk. He is a compass, who, however much you turn him this way and that, however you twist and twirl him, will always point north. We would go so far as to say that the importance of stewards, and indeed street-sweepers, to the proper functioning of the nations has yet to be studied. Now they are unloading the forage from the hold in which it has travelled alongside all the luxury items belonging to the archduke and the archduchess, but which, from now on, will be transported in carts chosen mainly for their functional nature, that is, being capable of accommodating the largest possible number of bundles. The water trough travels with the forage, but this time it is empty, since, as we will see, on the wintry roads of northern italy and austria, there will be no lack of water to fill it as often as proves necessary. Now it is time for the elephant suleiman to be disembarked. The noisy crowd of ordinary genoans is abuzz with impatience and excitement. If one were to ask these men and women who they were keenest to see close up, the archduke or the elephant, we think the elephant would win by a large margin. The eager expectation of this small multitude found release in a great roar, when, with his trunk, the elephant lifted onto his back a man carrying a small bag of belongings. It was subhro or fritz, depending on your preference, the carer, the keeper, the mahout, who had suffered such humiliation at the hands of the archduke and who now, in the eyes of the people of genoa gathered on the quay, will enjoy an almost perfect triumph. Seated on the elephant's shoulders, his bag between his legs, and dressed now in his grubby work clothes, he gazed down with all the arrogance of a conqueror at the people watching him open-mouthed, which, they say, is the most absolute sign of amazement, but which, perhaps because it is so absolute, is rarely, if ever, seen in real life. Whenever he was riding on solomon's back, the world always seemed small to subhro, but today, on the quay of the port of genoa, when he was the main focus of interest for the hundreds entranced by the spectacle before them, whether that consisted of his own person or the vast animal obeying his every order, fritz contemplated the crowd with a kind of scorn, and, in a rare flash of lucidity and relativity, it occurred to him that, all things considered, archdukes, kings and emperors were really nothing more than mahouts mounted on elephants. With a flick of his cane, he directed suleiman towards the gangway. Those members of the public who were closest drew back in alarm, even more so when the elephant, halfway down the gangway, and for reasons that will remain for ever unknown, decided to trumpet so loudly that, if you'll forgive the comparison, it sounded to their ears like the trumpets of jericho and sent the more fearful among them scattering. When it stepped onto the quay, though, perhaps as the result of an optical illusion, the elephant appeared to have suddenly shrunk in height and bulk. He still had to be viewed from below, but it was no longer necessary to lean back one's head quite so much. That is the effect of habit, the beast, while still of a terrifying size, seemed to the genoans to have lost its initial aura of eighth wonder of the sublunary world, now it was just an animal called an elephant, nothing more. Still full of his recent discovery about the nature of power and its supports, fritz was most displeased by the change that had taken place in the minds of the people, but the coup de grâce was still to be delivered by the emergence on deck of the archduke and archduchess, accompanied by their immediate entourage, and, above all, by the novel sight of two children being carried in the arms of two women, who doubtless were or still are their wetnurses. We can tell you now that one of these children, a little girl of two, will become the fourth wife of philip the second of spain and the first of portugal. As they say, small causes, large effects. We hope thus to satisfy the curiosity of those readers puzzled by the lack of information about the archduke and archduchess's numerous offspring, sixteen children, if you recall, of whom little ana was the first. As we were saying, the archduke had only to appear for there to be an explosion of applause and cheering, which he acknowledged with an indulgent wave of his gloved right hand. The archduke and archduchess did not use the gangway that had, until then, served as the unloading ramp, but another beside it, newly washed and scrubbed, in order

135

to avoid the slightest contact with any grime left behind by the horses' hooves, the elephant's huge legs or the bare feet of the longshoremen. We should congratulate the archduke on the efficiency of his steward, who has gone back on board to inspect the berths, just in case a diamond bracelet should have fallen down a gap between two floorboards. Outside, the cuirassiers waiting for his highness to descend have formed up into two tight lines so as to accommodate all the horses, twenty-five on either side. Now, if we did not fear committing a grave anachronism, we would like to imagine that the archduke walked to his carriage beneath a canopy of fifty unsheathed swords, however, it is more than likely that such acts of homage were thought up by some frivolous future century. The archduke and the arch-duchess have just stepped into the ornate, brilliant and yet sturdy carriage awaiting them. Now we only have to wait for the convoy to organise itself, with twenty cuirassiers in front to forge the way ahead and thirty behind to close it off, like a rapid intervention force, in the unlikely but not impossible event of an attack by bandits. True, we are not in calabria or sicily, but in the civilised lands of liguria, to be followed by lombardy and the veneto, but since, as popular wisdom has so often warned us, the fairest silk is soonest stained, the archduke is quite right to protect his rearguard. It remains to be seen what will fall from the heavens. Meanwhile, the transparent, luminous morning has gradually clouded over.

The rain was waiting for them as they left genoa. This is not so very odd, it is, after all, getting on for late autumn, and this downpour is merely the prelude to the concerto, with an ample array of tubas, percussion and trombones, that the alps is already holding in reserve to bestow on the convoy. Fortunately for those with fewest defences against the bad weather, we refer in particular to the cuirassiers and to the mahout, the former clothed in cold, uncomfortable steel, as if they were some kind of new-fangled beetle, the latter perched on top of the elephant, where the north winds and flailing snow are at their most cutting, maximilian finally paid heed to the infallible wisdom of the people, in this instance, to the saying that has been trotted out since the dawn of time, that prevention is better than cure. On the way out of genoa, he ordered the convoy to stop twice at shops selling ready-made clothes so that overcoats could be bought for the cuirassiers and for the mahout, said overcoats being, for understandable reasons, given the lack of planning in their production, disparate in both cut and colour, but at least they would protect their fortunate recipients. Thanks to this providential move on the part of the archduke, we can see the speed with which the soldiers removed the new greatcoats from the saddle trees on which they had been hung when distributed, and how, without pausing or dismounting, they put them on, displaying a military joy rarely seen in the history of armies. The mahout fritz, formerly known as subhro, did the same, albeit more discreetly. Snug inside the coat, it occurred to him that the saddle-cloth, so charitably returned to valladolid for the benefit of the bishop, would have been of great use to suleiman, who was being treated most uncharitably by the mountain rain. The result of the fierce storm that so swiftly followed on those first intermittent downpours, was that very few people came out onto the roads to welcome suleiman and to greet his highness. They were wrong not to do so, because they won't have another opportunity in the near future to see a real live elephant. As for the archduke, our uncertainty derives from our lack of information about any short trips which that almost imperial person might make, he might return, he might not. As for the elephant, though, we have no doubts, he will not travel these roads again. The weather cleared up even before they reached piacenza, which allowed them to cross the city in a manner that accorded better with the grandeur of the important people travelling in the convoy, for the cuirassiers were able to take off their coats and appear in all their familiar splendour, rather than continuing to cut the same ridiculous figure they had since leaving genoa, with warriors' helmets on their heads and coarse woollen greatcoats on their backs. This time, a lot of people came out onto the streets, and, while the archduke was applauded for who he was, the elephant was no less warmly applauded and for the same reason. Fritz had not taken off his coat. He felt that the generous cut of this rather crude apparel, more like a cape than a coat, gave him an air of sovereign dignity that fitted well with suleiman's majestic gait. To tell the truth, he didn't really care any more that the archduke had changed his name. Fritz, it is true, did not know the old saying, when in rome do as the romans do, but although he felt no inclination to be an austrian in austria, he thought it advisable, if he wanted to live a quiet life, to go unnoticed by the masses, even if their first sight of him was on the back of an elephant, which, right from the start, would make of him an exceptional being. Here he is then, wrapped in his greatcoat, delighting in the faint smell of billy-goat given off by the damp cloth. He was following the archduke's carriage, as he had been ordered to do when they left valladolid, and so anyone seeing him from afar would gain the impression that he was dragging after him the vast column of carts and wagons that made up the cortège, with, immediately behind him, the cart carrying the bundles of forage and the water trough that the rain had filled to overflowing. He was a happy mahout, far from the narrowness of his life in portugal, where they had pretty much left him to vegetate during those two years spent in the enclosure in belém, watching the ships set sail for india and listening to the chanting of the hieronymite friars. It's possible that our elephant is thinking, if that enormous head is capable of such a feat, it certainly doesn't lack for space, that he has reason to miss his former state of dolce far niente, but that could only occur thanks to his natural ignorance of the fact that indolence is highly prejudicial to the health. The one thing worse for it is tobacco, as people will find out later on. Now, however, after travelling three hundred leagues, mostly along roads that the devil himself, despite his cloven hooves, would refuse to take, suleiman could never be called indolent. He might have been called that during his stay in portugal, but that's all water under the bridge, he only had to set foot on the roads of europe to discover energies whose existence even he did not suspect. This phenomenon has often been observed in people who, due to circumstances, to poverty or unemployment, were forced to emigrate. Often indifferent and shiftless in the land where they were born, they become, almost from one hour to the next, as active and diligent as if they had the proverbial ants in their pants. Not even waiting for camp to be pitched on the outskirts of piacenza, suleiman is already asleep in the arms of the elephant's equivalent of morpheus. And fritz, beside him, covered by his coat, is sleeping the sleep of the just and snoring to boot. Early the next morning, the bugle sounded. It had rained during the night, but the sky was clear. Let us only hope that it doesn't fill up with grey clouds, as it did yesterday. Their nearest objective now is the city of mantua, in lombardy, which, though famous for many things, is perhaps best known as being home to one rigoletto, a certain jester at the duke's court, whose fortunes and misfortunes, much later on, will be set to music by the great giuseppe verdi. The convoy will not pause in mantua to appreciate the marvellous works of art that abound in that city. There will be more in verona, a city that will be the backdrop chosen by william shakespeare for his most excellent and lamentable tragedy of romeo and juliet, and where, given the settled weather, the archduke has ordered them to proceed not because maximilian the second of austria is particularly interested in any other loves than his own, but because verona, if we don't count padua, will be their last major stop before venice, after that, it will be one long climb in the direction of the alps, towards the cold north. Apparently, the archduke and archduchess have already visited, on previous journeys, the beautiful city of the doges, where, on the other hand, it would be no easy matter to accommodate suleiman's four tons, always assuming that they were thinking of taking him with them as a mascot. An elephant is hardly an animal that could be fitted into a gondola, if gondolas existed then, at least in their current design, with the raised prow and painted the funereal black that distinguishes them from all other navies in the world, and there would certainly have been no singing gondolier at the stern. The archduke and archduchess might decide to take a turn along the grand canal and be received by the doge, but suleiman, the cuirassiers and the rest of the cortège will remain in padua, facing the basilica of St Anthony, whom we hereby reclaim as rightfully belonging to lisbon not to padua, in a space bare of trees and other vegetation. Keeping everything in its place will always be the best way of achieving world peace, unless divine wisdom disposes otherwise.

It happened, early the following morning, when the soldiers were still barely awake, that an emissary from the basilica of St Anthony appeared in the camp. He had, he said, although not perhaps in these exact words, been sent by a superior of the church's ecclesiastical team to speak to the man in charge of the elephant. Now any object three metres high can be seen from some distance away, and suleiman almost filled the celestial vault, but, even so, the priest asked to be taken to him. The cuirassier who accompanied him shook the mahout awake, for he was still asleep, snug in his greatcoat. There's a priest here to see you, he said. He chose to speak in castilian, and that was the best thing he could have done, given that the mahout's as yet limited grasp of the german language was not sufficient for him to understand such a complex sentence. Fritz opened his mouth to ask what the priest wanted, but immediately closed it again, preferring not to create a linguistic confusion that might lead him who knows where. He got up and went over to the priest who was waiting at a prudent distance, You wish to speak to me, father, he asked, Indeed, I do, my son, replied his visitor, putting into those five words all the warmth of feeling he could muster, How can I help you, father, Are you a christian, came the question, I was baptised, but as you can see from my complexion and my features, I am not from here, No, I assume you're an indian, but that is no impediment to your being a good christian, That is not for me to say, for, as I understand it, self-praise is a shameful thing, Now, I have come to make a request, but first, I would like to know if your elephant is trained, Well, he's not trained in the sense that he can perform circus tricks, but he usually comports himself in as dignified a fashion as any self-respecting elephant, Could you make him kneel down, even if only on one knee, That is something I've never tried, father, but I have noticed that suleiman does kneel motu proprio when he wants to lie down, but I can't be certain that he would do so to order, You could try, This is not the best time, father, suleiman tends to be rather bad-tempered in the morning, If it would be more convenient, I can come back later, for what brings me here is certainly not a life-or-death affair, although it would be very much in the interests of the basilica if it were to happen today, before his highness the archduke of austria leaves for the north, If what happens today, if you don't mind my asking, The miracle, said the priest, putting his hands together, What miracle, asked the mahout, feeling his head beginning to spin, If the elephant were to kneel down at the door of the basilica, would that not seem to you a miracle, one of the great miracles of our age, asked the priest, again putting his hands together in prayer, I know nothing of miracles, where I come from there have been no miracles since the world was created, for the creation, I imagine, must have been one long miracle, but then that was that, So you are not a christian, That's for you to decide, father, but even though I was anointed a christian and baptised, perhaps you can still see what lies beneath, And what does lie beneath, Ganesh, for example, our elephant god, that one over there, flapping his ears, and you will doubtless ask me how I know that suleiman the elephant is a god, and I will respond that if there is, as there is, an elephant god, it could as easily be him as another, Given that I need you to do me a favour, I forgive you these blasphemies, but, when this is over, you will have to confess, And what favour do you want from me, father, To take the elephant to the door of the basilica and make him kneel down there, But I'm not sure I can do that, Try, Imagine if I take the elephant there and he refuses to kneel down, now I may not know much about these things, but I assume that even worse than no miracle would be a failed miracle, It won't have failed if there are witnesses, And who will those witnesses be, First of all, the whole of the basilica's religious community and as many willing christians as we can gather at the entrance to the church, secondly, the public, who, as we know, are capable of swearing that they saw what they didn't and stating as fact what they don't know, And does that include believing in miracles that never happened, asked the mahout, They're usually the best ones, and although they involve a lot of preparation, the effort is usually worth it, besides, that way we relieve our saints of some of their duties, And god as well, We never pester god for miracles, one has to respect the hierarchy, at most, we consult the virgin, who also has a gift for working miracles, There seems to be a strong vein of cynicism in your catholic church, Possibly, but the reason I'm speaking so frankly, said the priest, is so that you will see how much we need this miracle, this or another, Why, Because luther, even though he's dead, is still stirring up a lot of prejudice against our holy religion, and anything that will help

143

us curtail the effects of protestant preaching will be welcome, remember, it's only thirty years since he nailed his vile theses to the door of the castle church in wittenberg, and since then, protestantism has swept through the whole of europe like a flood, Look, I don't know anything about those theses or whatever, You don't need to, you just need to have faith, Faith in god or in my elephant, asked the mahout, In both, replied the priest, And what do I stand to gain from this, One does not ask things of the church, one gives, In that case, you should speak to the elephant first, since the success of the miracle depends on him, Be careful, you have a most impertinent tongue, mind you don't lose it, And what will happen to me if I take the elephant to the door of the basilica and he doesn't kneel down, Nothing, unless we suspect that you're to blame, And if I was, You would have good reason to repent. The mahout thought it best to give in, At what time do you want me to bring you the animal, he asked, At midday on the dot, not a minute later, Well, I hope I have enough time to get the idea into suleiman's head that he must kneel at your feet, Not at our feet, for we are unworthy, but at the feet of our saint anthony, and with those pious words, the priest went off to tell his superiors the results of his evangelical work, Is there any hope of success, they asked, Very much so, even though we are in the hands of an elephant, Elephants don't have hands, That was just a manner of speaking, like saying, for example, that we're in the hands of god, The main difference being that we are in the hands of god, Praised be his name, Indeed, but getting back to the point, why exactly are we in the elephant's hands, Because we don't know what he will do when he arrives at the door of the basilica, He'll do whatever the mahout tells him to do, that's what education is for, Let us trust in god's benevolent understanding of the facts of this world, if god, as we suppose, wants to be served, it will suit him to help his own miracles, those that will best speak of his glory, Brothers, faith can do anything, and god will do what is necessary, Amen, they chorused, mentally preparing an arsenal of auxiliary prayers.

Meanwhile, fritz was trying, by all possible means, to get the elephant to understand what was required of him. This was no easy task for an animal of firm opinions, who immediately associated the action of kneeling with the subsequent action of lying down to sleep. Little by little, though, after many blows, innumerable oaths and a few desperate pleas, light began to dawn in suleiman's hitherto obstinate brain, namely, that he had to kneel, but not lie down. Fritz even went so far as to say, My life is in your hands, which just goes to show how ideas can spread, not only directly, by word of mouth, but simply because they hang about in the atmospheric currents around us, constituting, you might say, a veritable bath in which one learns things quite without realising. Given the scarcity of clocks, what counted then was the height of the sun and the length of the shadow it cast on the ground. That is how fritz knew that midday was approaching and, therefore, the moment to lead the elephant to the door of the basilica, and then it would all be up to god. There he goes, riding on suleiman's back, just as we have seen him do before, but now his hands and heart are trembling, as if he were a mere apprentice mahout. He need not have worried. When he reached the door of the basilica, before a crowd of witnesses who will, for ever after, confirm that the miracle occurred, the elephant, obeying a light touch to his right ear, bent his knees, not just one, which would have been enough to satisfy the priest who came with the request, but both, thus bowing to the majesty of god in heaven and to his representatives on earth. Suleiman received in return a generous sprinkling of holy water that even reached the mahout on top, while the watching crowd, as one, fell to their knees, and a shiver of pleasure ran through glorious saint anthony's mummified corpse where it lay in his tomb.

That same afternoon, two carrier-pigeons, one male and one female, set off from the basilica in the direction of trent, taking with them the news of this marvellous miracle. Why trent and not rome, where the head of the church is to be found, you will ask. The answer is simple, because, since fifteen forty-five, an ecumenical council has been taking place in trent, engaged, according to them, in preparing a counter-attack on luther and his followers. Suffice it to say that decrees had already been issued on the sacred scriptures and tradition, on original sin, justification and the sacraments in general. It is understandable, therefore, that the basilica of saint anthony, a pillar of the faith at its purest, needs to be kept permanently informed about what is going on in trent, which is so close, only twenty leagues away, a mere vol d'oiseau, appropriately enough, for pigeons, who have been flying between the two locations for years. This time, however, padua is the first with the news, because it isn't every day that an elephant solemnly kneels at the door of a basilica, thus bearing witness to the fact that the message of the gospels is addressed to the whole animal kingdom and that the regrettable drowning of those hundreds of pigs in the sea of galilee could be put down to inexperience, occurring as it did before the cogs in the mechanism for performing miracles were properly oiled. What matters now are the long queues of believers forming in the encampment, all eager to see the elephant and take advantage of the chance to buy a tuft of elephant hair, a business rapidly set up by fritz when the payment he naïvely assumed he would receive from the basilica's coffers was not forthcoming.

Let us not censure the mahout, for others who did far less for the christian faith were nonetheless amply rewarded. Tomorrow it will be claimed that an infusion of elephant hair taken three times a day is a sovereign remedy for cases of acute diarrhoea and that if the same tuft of hair is soaked in almond oil and the oil massaged energetically into the scalp, again three times a day, it will halt even the most galloping of alopecias. Fritz can barely cope with the demand, the purse tied to his belt is already heavy with coins, if the camp were to stay there a whole week, he would be a rich man. His customers are not all from padua, some are from mestre and even venice. It is said that the archduke and archduchess are having such a good time at the doge's palace that they will not return today, or even tomorrow, a piece of news that makes fritz very happy, indeed, he never thought he would have so many reasons to feel grateful to the house of habsburg. He wonders why it had never occurred to him before to sell elephant hair when he lived in india and then he thinks to himself that, despite the ridiculous number of deities, subdeities and demons infesting that country, there are far fewer superstitions in the land where he was born than in this particular part of civilised and very christian europe, which is capable of blithely buying some elephant hair and piously believing the vendor's lies. Having to pay for your own dreams must be the most desperate of situations. In the end, contrary to the prognostications of the so-called barracks gazette, the archduke and archduchess returned on the afternoon of the following day, ready to resume their journey as soon as possible. News of the miracle had reached the doge's palace, but in somewhat garbled form, the result of the successive transmissions of facts, true or assumed, real or purely imaginary, based on everything from partial, more or less eye-witness accounts to reports from those who simply liked the sound of their own voice, for, as we know all too well, no one telling a story can resist adding a full stop, and sometimes even a comma. The archduke summoned his steward to clarify what had happened, not so much the miracle itself, but the reasons that had led to it. On this particular matter, the steward lacked sufficient information, and so it was decided to summon the mahout fritz, who, given the nature of his role, should have something more substantial to tell. The archduke did not beat about the bush, They tell me that a miracle took place during my absence, Yes, sir, And that suleiman was involved, That is so, sir, You mean that the elephant decided, of his own volition, to go and kneel at the door of the basilica, That isn't quite how I would put it, sir, How would you put it, then, asked the archduke, Sir, I was the one who took suleiman there, So I thought, although that's not what interests me, what I want to know is in whose head was the idea born, All I had to do, sir, was to teach the elephant to kneel at my command, And who gave you the order to do so, Sir, I'm not allowed to discuss the matter, Did someone forbid you to, Not exactly, but a word to the wise is enough, And who proffered you that word, Forgive me, sir, but, If you don't answer my question at once you will have reason to regret it most bitterly, It was a priest from the basilica, And what did he say, He said that they needed a miracle and that suleiman could provide that miracle, And what did you answer, That suleiman wasn't used to performing miracles and that the attempt might result in failure, And what was the priest's response, He said that I would have reason to repent if I didn't obey, almost the same words that your highness just used, And then what happened, Well, I spent the rest of the morning teaching suleiman to kneel at a signal from me, which wasn't easy, but I managed it in the end, You're a good mahout, You're too kind, sir, Would you like some advice, Yes, sir, Don't tell anyone else about our conversation, No, sir, That way you'll have no reason to regret anything, Right, sir, I won't forget, Off you go and be sure to remove from suleiman's head the idiotic idea that he can go around performing miracles by kneeling down at the doors of churches, one expects much more from a miracle, for example, that someone should grow a new leg to replace one that was cut off, imagine the number of such prodigies that could be performed on the battlefield, Yes, sir, Off you go. Once alone, the archduke began to think that perhaps he had said too much, that his words, if the mahout let his tongue run away with him, would be of no benefit whatsoever to the delicate political balance he has been trying to keep between luther's reforms and the on-going conciliar response. After all, as henry the fourth of france will say in the not too distant future, paris is well worth a mass. Even so, a look of painful melancholy appears on maximilian's slender face, perhaps because few things in life hurt as much as the awareness that one has betrayed the ideas of one's youth. The archduke told himself that he was old enough not to cry over spilt milk, that the superabundant udders of the catholic church were there, as always, waiting for a pair of skilful hands to milk them, and events so far had shown that his archducal hands had a certain talent for that diplomatic milking, as long as the said church believed that the results of those matters of faith would, in time, bring them some advantage. Even so, the story of the elephant's false miracle went beyond the bounds of what was tolerable. The people at the basilica, he thought, must have gone mad, after all, they already had a saint who could make a new pitcher out of the fragments of a broken one and who, while living in padua, was able to fly through the air to lisbon to save his father from the gallows, why then go and ask a mahout to get his elephant to fake a miracle, ah, luther, luther, you were so right. Having vented his feelings, the archduke summoned his steward, whom he ordered to prepare for departure the following morning, travelling, if possible, directly to trent or, if necessary, spending at most one night encamped en route. The steward replied that he thought the second option more prudent, for experience had shown that they could not count on suleiman when it came to speed, He's more of a long-distance runner, he concluded, adding, The mahout has been taking advantage of people's credulity and is selling them elephant hair so that they can make potions that won't cure anyone, Tell him from me that if he doesn't cease doing so this instant he will have reason to regret it for the rest of his life, which will certainly not be a long one, Your highness' orders will be carried out at once, we have to put a stop to this fraud as quickly as possible, this elephant hair business is demoralising the whole convoy, especially the balder members of the cuirassiers, Right, I want this matter resolved, I can't prevent suleiman's so-called miracle pursuing us for the rest of the journey, but at least no one will be able to say that the house of habsburg is prof-iting from the crimes of a lying mahout and collecting value added tax as if it were a commercial operation covered by the law, Sir, I will deal with the matter forthwith, he'll be laughing on the other side of his face when I've finished, it's just a shame that we need him to get the elephant to vienna, but I hope, at least, that this will teach him a lesson, Go on, put out that fire before anyone gets burned. Fritz did not really deserve such harsh judgements. It's only right that the criminal should be accused and condemned, but true justice should always bear in mind any extenuating circumstances, the first of which, in the mahout's case, would be that the idea of the fake miracle came not from him, but from the priests of the basilica of saint anthony, who thought up the hoax in the first place, if they hadn't, it would never have occurred to fritz that he could grow rich by exploiting the capillary system of the maker of that apparent miracle. In recognition of their own greater and lesser sins, given that no one in this world is blameless, and they far less than most, both the noble archduke and his obliging steward had a duty to remember that famous saying about the beam and the mote, which, adapted to these new circumstances, teaches how much easier it is to see the beam in your neighbour's eye than the elephant's hair in your own. Besides, this is not a miracle that will linger long in people's memories or in those of future generations. Contrary to the archduke's fears, the story of the false miracle will not pursue them for the rest of the journey and will quickly fade. The people in the convoy, both noble and plebeian, military and civilian, will have far more to think about when the clouds building up over the region around trent, above the mountains that immediately precede the wall of the alps, become, first, rain, then possibly hard-hitting hail and, doubtless, snow, and the roads become covered in slippery ice. And then it is likely that some members of the convoy will recognise, at last, that the poor elephant was nothing but an innocent dupe in that grotesque entry in the church's accounting records and that the mahout is merely an insignificant product of the corrupt times in which we happen to live. Farewell, world, you go from worse to worse.

Despite the archduke's express wishes, it was impossible to cover the distance between padua and trent in one day. Suleiman tried his hardest to obey the mahout's urgent commands, indeed the mahout seemed determined to take it out on him for the failure of a business that had begun so well and ended so badly, but elephants, even those who weigh four tons, also have their physical limits. In fact, it all turned out for the best. Instead of reaching their destination in the half-light of evening, in near-darkness, they arrived in trent at midday, when they were greeted by people in the streets and by applause. The sky was still covered from horizon to horizon by what seemed like solid cloud, but it wasn't raining. The convoy's meteorologists, who are, by vocation, the majority, were unanimous, It's going to snow, they said, and hard. When the cortège reached trent, a surprise was awaiting them in the square outside the cathedral of saint vigilius. In the exact centre of that square stood a more or less half life-size statue of an elephant, or, rather, a construction made out of planks that bore every appearance of having been hastily nailed together, with little attempt to achieve anatomical exactitude, although they had included a raised trunk and a pair of tusks, the ivory of which was represented by a lick of white paint, this, one assumes, was intended to represent suleiman, well, it must have, since no other animal of his species was expected in that part of the country nor was there any record of another elephant having visited trent, not at least in the recent past. When the archduke saw the elephantoid figure, he trembled. His worst fears were confirmed, news of the miracle had clearly arrived in trent, and the religious authorities of the city, which had already benefited, materially and spiritually, from the fact that the council was being held within its walls, had found confirmation of, how shall we put it, a kind of shared sanctity with padua and the basilica of saint anthony, and had decided to demonstrate this by erecting a hasty construction representing the miracle-working creature in front of the very cathedral where the cardinals, bishops and theologians had been meeting now for years. When he took a closer look, the archduke noticed that there were large holes in the elephant's back, rather like trapdoors, which immediately made him think of the celebrated trojan horse, although it was perfectly clear that there wouldn't be room in the statue's belly for even a squadron of children, unless they were lilliputians, but that was impossible, because the word hadn't even been invented yet. To clarify the situation, the anxious archduke ordered his steward to go and find out what the devil that worrying, cobbled-together monstrosity was doing there. The steward went and returned. There was no reason to be alarmed. The elephant had been created in order to celebrate maximilian of austria's visit to the city of trent, and its other purpose, and this was true, was as a frame for the fireworks that would erupt from the wooden carcass when darkness fell. The archduke gave a sigh of relief, the elephant's actions were obviously deemed to be of little importance in trent, apart, perhaps, from providing an object capable of being burned to a cinder, for there was a strong likelihood that the fuses attached to the fireworks would ignite the wood, providing spectators with a finale that would, many years later, merit the adjective wagnerian. And so it was. After a storm of colours, in which the yellow of sodium, the red of calcium, the green of copper, the blue of potassium, the white of magnesium and the gold of iron all performed miracles, in which stars, fountains, slow-burning candles and cascades of lights poured out of the elephant as if from an inexhaustible cornucopia, the celebrations ended with a huge bonfire around which many of trent's inhabitants would take the opportunity to stand and warm their hands, while suleiman, in the shelter of a lean-to built for the purpose, was finishing off his second bundle of forage. The fire was gradually becoming a glowing heap of embers, but this did not last long in the cold, and the embers rapidly turned into ashes, although by then, once the main spectacle was over, the archduke and the archduchess had both retired to bed. The snow began to fall.

There are the alps. Yes, there they are, but you can hardly see them. The snow is falling softly, like scraps of cotton wool, but that softness is deceiving, as our elephant will tell you, for he is carrying on his back an ever more visible layer of ice, which the mahout should have noticed by now, were it not for the fact that he is from a hot country where this kind of winter is almost unimaginable. Of course in old india, in the north, there is no shortage of mountains and snowy peaks, but subhro, now known as fritz, never had the money to travel for his own pleasure and to see other places. His one experience of snow was in lisbon, a few weeks after arriving from goa, when, one cold night, he saw falling from the sky a white dust, like flour being sieved, which melted as soon as it touched the ground. Nothing like the white vastness before his eyes now, stretching for as far as he can see. Very soon, the scraps of cotton wool had become large, heavy flakes which, driven by the wind, beat against the mahout's face. Sitting astride suleiman and wrapped in his greatcoat, fritz did not feel the cold particularly, but those continuous, endless blows to the face troubled him as if they were some kind of dangerous threat. He had been told that from trent to bolzano was a mere stroll, some ten leagues, or a little less, a flea-jump away, but not in this weather, when the snow seemed to be possessed of claws with which to grasp and delay any and every movement, even breathing, as if unwilling to allow the imprudent traveller to leave, as suleiman knows, for despite the strength given him by nature, he can only drag himself painfully up those steep paths. We do not know what he is thinking, but, in the midst of these alps, we can be sure of one thing, he is not a happy elephant. Apart from the occasions when the cuirassiers ride past as best they can on their frozen mounts, up hill and down hill, to see how the convoy is coping and to avoid any dispersals or diversions that could mean death to anyone who might lose their way in that icy place, the path seems to exist only for the elephant and his mahout. Having grown used, since their departure from valladolid, to being close to the carriage carrying the archduke and archduchess, the mahout misses seeing it there before him, although we dare not speak for the elephant because, as we said earlier, we do not know what he is thinking. The archducal carriage is somewhere up ahead, but there is no sign of it, nor of the cart laden with forage, which should be following immediately behind them. The mahout looked back to see if this was so, and that providential glance made him notice the layer of ice covering suleiman's hindquarters. Although he knew nothing of winter sports, it seemed to him that the ice was fairly thin and fragile, probably due to the heat from the animal's body, which would not allow the ice to set completely. At least that's something, he thought. However, before things got any worse, he needed to remove it. Taking infinite care, so as not to slip, the mahout crawled along the elephant's back until he reached the offending sheet of ice, which turned out to be neither as thin nor as fragile as had at first seemed. One should never trust ice, that is the first important lesson to learn. Stepping onto a frozen sea might give others the impression that we can walk on water, but it is an entirely false one, as false as the miracle of suleiman kneeling at the door of the basilica of saint anthony, for suddenly the ice gives way and who knows what will happen then. Fritz's problem now is how to remove that wretched ice from the elephant's skin without recourse to some kind of tool, a spatula with a fine, rounded blade, for example, would be ideal, but there are no such spatulas to be had, if, indeed, such things existed then. The only solution, therefore, is to use his bare hands, and we are not speaking figuratively. The mahout's fingers were already numb with cold when he realised where the nub of the problem lay, namely, that the elephant's thick, coarse hair had made common cause with the ice, so that any small advance was won only after a desperate battle, for just as there was no spatula to help scrape the ice off the skin, so there were no scissors with which to cut that hairy tangle. It quickly became clear that removing each hair from the ice was far beyond fritz's physical and mental capabilities, and he was obliged to abandon the task before he himself turned into a pathetic snowman, lacking only a pipe in his mouth and a carrot instead of a nose. The very same hairs that had been at the heart of a promising business, nipped in the bud by the archduke's moral scruples, were now the cause of a fiasco whose consequences to the elephant's health were as yet unknown. As if this were not enough, another apparently urgent matter had just arisen. Disconcerted to feel that the mahout's familiar weight had transferred from his shoulders to his hindquarters, the elephant was showing clear signs of disorientation, as if he had lost sight of the path and did not know where to go. Fritz had no alternative but to scramble rapidly back to his accustomed place and, so to speak, take up the reins again. As for the covering of ice on the elephant's back, let us pray to the god of elephants that nothing worse happens. If there was a tree nearby with a really strong branch three metres up and more or less parallel to the ground, suleiman could free himself from that uncomfortable and possibly dangerous sheet of ice, by rubbing against it, as all elephants have done since time immemorial, whenever an itch became unbearable. Now that the snow had redoubled in intensity, although this is not to say that one was a consequence of the other, the road had grown steeper, as if it were weary of dragging itself along on the flat and wanted to ascend to the skies, even if only to one of its lower levels. Just as the wings of the humming-bird cannot even dream of the powerful beating of the petrel's wings as it battles against the stormy wind nor of the majestic flight of the golden eagle as it soars above the valleys. Each of us is made for the thing for which we were born, but there is always the possibility that we might encounter important exceptions, as was the case with suleiman, who was not born for this, but whose only option was to invent some way of coping with that steep incline, which he did by stretching out his trunk in front of him, looking every inch the warrior charging into battle to meet either death or glory. And all around is snow and solitude. Someone who knows the region might say that this whiteness conceals a landscape of extraordinary beauty. But no one would think so, least of all us. The snow devoured the valleys, buried the vegetation, and if there are any inhabited houses around, they can barely be seen, a little smoke from a chimney is the only sign of life, someone inside must have lit some damp kindling and is now waiting, with the door practically blocked by a snowdrift, for the aid of a saint bernard with a barrel of brandy tied round its neck. Almost without his noticing, suleiman had reached the top of the slope, and he can now breathe normally again and, after all that sheer painful effort, especially with a mahout on his back and a sheet of ice weighing on his hindquarters, can resume an easy walking pace. The curtain of snow had thinned slightly, allowing one to see a few hundred metres of path ahead, as if the world had decided, at last, to restore the lost meteorological norm. Perhaps that really was what the world intended, but something odd has obviously happened, how else explain this gathering of people, horses and carts, as if they had come upon a good place for a picnic. Fritz urged suleiman to quicken his step and saw that he was back once more among his companions and the convoy, which, it must be said, did not take much perspicacity because, as we know, there is only one archduke of austria. Fritz climbed down from the elephant and the question he asked of the first person he met, What happened, received an instant reply, The front axle of his highness' coach has broken, How dreadful, exclaimed the mahout, The carpenter is already installing a new axle with the help of his assistants, and we'll be ready to head off again within the hour, How come they had one with them, One what, An axle, You may know a lot about elephants, but it obviously hasn't occurred to you that no one would risk setting out on a journey like this without taking with them some spare parts, And were their highnesses injured at all, No, they just got a bit of a fright when the coach suddenly lurched to one side, Where are they now, Taking shelter in another coach, further on, It will be night soon, With heavy snow like this, the road is always light, no one will get lost, said the sergeant of the cuirassiers, who was the man he was speaking to. And it was true because, at that moment, the cart carrying the forage arrived, and just in time too, because suleiman, having dragged his four tons up those mountains, desperately needed to recharge his energies. In less time than it takes to say amen, fritz had untied two of the bundles right there, and a second amen, if there was one, found the elephant eagerly munching his ration of food. Immediately behind came the cuirassiers from the rear of the convoy and with them the rest of the company, numb with cold and exhausted by the tremendous efforts they'd been obliged to make for leagues and leagues, but glad to rejoin the group. When one thinks about it, the accident to the archducal coach could only have been an act of divine providence. As that never sufficiently praised popular wisdom teaches us, and as has more than once been shown, god writes straight on crooked lines, and even seems to prefer the latter. When the axle had been replaced and the soundness of the repair tested, the archduke and archduchess returned to the comfort of their coach, and the convoy, fully regrouped, set off, with strict orders having been issued to all its members, both military and civilian, to keep together at all costs and not to slide again into the same state of almost total fragmentation, which had only avoided the direst of consequences thanks to the greatest of good fortune. It was late at night when the convoy reached bolzano.

The following day, the convoy slept in until late, the archduke and archduchess in the house of a local family of nobles, the others scattered here and there throughout the small town of bolzano, the cuirassiers' horses distributed among whichever stables still had room, and the men billeted in private houses, because camping outside would have been a most unappealing prospect, if not impossible, unless the company still had strength enough to spend the rest of the night clearing snow. The hardest task was to find a billet for suleiman. After looking high and low, they found a kind of shelter, a tiled roof supported by four pillars, which offered him little more protection than if he were to sleep à la belle étoile, which is the lyrical french version of the portuguese expression ao relento, although that is equally inappropriate, really, because relento means the night damp, a kind of dew or mist, meteorological trifles when compared with these alpine snows that would easily justify such poetical descriptions as spotless blanket or mortal bed. There he was left no fewer than three bundles of forage to satisfy his appetite, whether there and then or during the night, for suleiman is as subject to his appetite as any human being. As for the mahout, he was lucky enough, when lodgings were being allocated, to be given a merciful mattress on the floor and a no less merciful blanket, whose calorific power was increased when he spread his greatcoat on top, even though said coat was still somewhat damp. The family who took him in had but one room with three beds, one for the mother and father, another for their three boys, aged between nine and fourteen, and the third for the septuagenarian grandmother and the two maids. The only payment they demanded of fritz was that he tell them some stories about elephants, which fritz was glad to do, beginning with his pièce de résistance, namely, the birth of ganesh, and finishing with the recent, and in his view, heroic ascent of the alps of which, we believe, quite enough has been said. Then the father, from his bed, while his wife lay snoring beside him, mentioned that, according to ancient histories and subsequent legends, the famous carthaginian general, hannibal, having crossed the pyrenees, had marched through more or less this same region of the alps with his army of men and african elephants, who had given the soldiers of rome such a hard time, although more modern versions state that they were not really african elephants, with huge ears and vast bodies, but so-called forest elephants, not much bigger than horses. But there were heavy snowfalls then too, he added, and no clear paths to follow either, You don't seem to like the romans very much, said fritz, The truth is that we're more austrian than italian here, in german our town is called bozen, To be honest, I prefer bolzano, said the mahout, it's easier on the ear, That's because you're portuguese, Having travelled from portugal doesn't make me portuguese, Where are you from then, sir, if you don't mind my asking, I was born in india and I'm a mahout, A mahout, Yes, mahout is the name given to people who drive elephants, In that case, the carthaginian general must have had mahouts in his army too, He wouldn't be able to take elephants anywhere if he didn't have someone to drive them, He took them to war, To a war waged by men, Well, there isn't really any other kind. The man was a philosopher.

Late the next morning, his strength restored and his stomach more or less consoled, fritz thanked the family for their hospitality and went to see if he still had an elephant to look after. He had dreamed that suleiman had left bolzano at dead of night and wandered off into the surrounding mountains and valleys, in the grip of a kind of intoxication that could only have been the effect of the snow, although the bibliography on the subject, with the exception of hannibal's disasters of war in the alps, has, in more recent times, been limited to recording, with tedious monotony, the broken legs and arms of those who love skiing. Yes, those were the days, when a person would fall from the top of a mountain and arrive, splat, a thousand metres below, at the bottom of a valley already crammed with the ribs, tibia and skulls of other equally unfortunate adventurers. Ah, yes, that was the life. A few cuirassiers were already gathered in the square, some on horseback, others not, and the rest were arriving to join them. It was snowing, but only lightly. Ever curious, out of necessity, given that no one bothered to tell him anything directly, the mahout went to ask the sergeant what was happening. He needed to say only a polite good morning, because the sergeant, knowing at once what he wanted, told him the latest news, We're going to bressanone, or brixen, as we say in german, it will be a short journey today, less than ten leagues. Then, after a pause intended to arouse expectation, he added, Apparently, in brixen, we're going to get a few days of much-needed rest, Well, I can only speak for myself, but suleiman can barely put one foot in front of the other, this is no climate for him, he might catch pneumonia and I'd like to see what his highness would do then with the poor creature's bones, It'll be all right, said the sergeant, things haven't gone so badly up to now. Fritz had no option but to agree and then he went to see how suleiman was. He found him in his shelter, apparently perfectly calm, but the mahout, still under the spell of that uncomfortable dream, couldn't escape the feeling that suleiman was pretending, as if he really had left bolzano in the middle of the night to romp around in the snows, perhaps climbing to the highest peaks, where the snow, they say, is eternal. On the ground there wasn't a trace of the food they had left him, not even a piece of straw, which at least meant that they could reasonably expect that he wouldn't start whining with hunger as small children do, even though, and this is not widely known, he, the elephant, is really another kind of child, not in his physical make-up, but as regards his imperfect intellect. In fact, we don't know what the elephant is thinking, but then we don't know what a child is thinking either, apart from what the child chooses to tell us, and one shouldn't, on principle, place too much trust in that. Fritz signalled that he wanted to get on, and the elephant, quickly and precisely as if wanting to be forgiven for some mischief, offered him one tusk to rest his foot on, just as if it were a stirrup, then coiled his trunk around his body, like an embrace. In one movement, he lifted fritz onto his back, where he left him comfortably installed. Fritz glanced behind him, and, contrary to his expectations, found not the slightest trace of ice on his hindquarters. Therein lay a mystery that he would probably never be able to solve. Either the elephant, any elephant and this one in particular, has some kind of self-regulating heating system capable, after a necessary period of mental concentration, of melting a reasonably thick layer of ice, or else the effort of going up and down mountains at some speed had caused the aforesaid ice to detach itself from his skin despite the labyrinthine tangle of hairs that had given fritz so much grief. Some of nature's mysteries seem, at first sight, impenetrable, and prudence perhaps counsels us to leave them be, in case a piece of raw knowledge should bring us more bad than good. Just look, for example, at what happened to adam in paradise when he ate what appeared to be an ordinary apple. It may be that the fruit itself was a delicious piece of work by god, although there are those who say that it wasn't an apple at all, but a slice of water melon, but, in either case, the seeds had been placed there by the devil. They were black after all.

The archducal coach is waiting for its noble, illustrious, distinguished passengers. Fritz directs the elephant to the place reserved for him in the cortège, behind the coach, but at a prudent distance, not wishing to anger the archduke by the near presence of a trickster like him, who, while not going to the classic extreme of selling a pig in a poke, had nevertheless duped a few poor bald men, among them some brave cuirassiers, with the promise that their hair would grow as thick as the hair of that unfortunate, mythic figure, samson. He need not have worried, the archduke didn't even look in his direction, he seemed to have other things on his mind, he wanted to reach bressanone before nightfall and they were already late. He despatched the aide-de-camp to take his orders to the head of the convoy, orders that could be summarised in three almost synonymous words, speed, alacrity, haste, allowing, of course, for the delaying effects of the snow that had begun to fall more thickly now, and the state of the roads, which, normally bad, were now even worse. It may only be a journey of ten leagues, as the helpful sergeant had informed the mahout, but if, by current calculations, ten leagues are fifty thousand metres or some tens of thousands of paces in old measurements, there's no avoiding the facts, numbers are numbers, then the people and animals who have just set off for yet another painful day's journeying are going to suffer greatly, especially those who are not blessed with a roof, which is most of them. How pretty the snow looks seen through the glass, the archduchess maria remarked ingenuously to her husband, the archduke maximilian, but for those of us outside, our eyes blinded by the wind and our boots sodden with snow, with the chilblains on our hands and feet burning like the fires of hell, it would be timely to ask the heavens just what we did to deserve such a punishment. As the poet said, the pine trees may wave at the sky, but the sky does not answer. It doesn't answer men either, even though most of them have known the right prayers since they were children, the problem is finding a language that god can understand. They say that the cold, when it's born, is intended for everyone, but some get more than their fair share of it. There is a vast difference between travelling in a coach lined with furs and blankets fitted with a thermostat and having to walk along in the flailing snow or with your foot in a frozen stirrup that feels, in the cold, as tight as a tourniquet. What did cheer them up was the news the sergeant had passed on to fritz about the possibility of having a good rest in bressanone, news that spread like a spring breeze throughout the convoy, but then the pessimists, singly and altogether, reminded the forgetful of the dangers of the isarco pass, not to mention another still worse that lies ahead, in austrian territory, the brenner pass. Had hannibal dared to go through either, we would probably not have had to wait for the battle of zama in order to watch, at our local cinema, the last, definitive defeat of the carthaginian army by scipio africanus, a film about the romans produced by benito's eldest son, vittorio mussolini. On that occasion, the elephants proved of no use to the great hannibal.

Mounted on suleiman's shoulders and receiving in his face the full brunt of the snow being whipped up by the incessant wind, fritz is not in the best of positions to elaborate and develop elevated thoughts. Nevertheless, he keeps trying to think of ways to improve his relations with the archduke, who not only refuses to speak to him, he won't even look at him. Things had begun rather well in valladolid, but suleiman, with his intestinal upsets on the way to rosas, had seriously damaged the noble cause of creating harmony between two social classes as far removed from one another as mahouts and archdukes. With a little good will, all this could have been forgotten, but the offence committed by subhro or fritz or whoever the devil he is, the madness that had made him want to grow rich by illicit and morally reprehensible means, put paid to any hopes of restoring the almost fraternal esteem which, for one magical moment, had brought the future emperor of austria closer to that humble driver of elephants. The sceptics are quite right when they say that the history of humanity is one long succession of missed opportunities. Fortunately, thanks to the inexhaustible generosity of the imagination, we erase faults, fill in lacunae as best we can, forge passages through blind alleys that will remain stubbornly blind, and invent keys to doors that have never even had locks. This is what fritz is doing while suleiman, painfully lifting his heavy legs, one, two, one, two, makes his way through the snow that continues to accumulate on the path, while the pure water out of which it is made insidiously transforms itself into the slipperiest of ice. Fritz thinks bitterly that only an act of heroism on his part would restore him to the archduke's favours, but, however hard he tries, he can come up with nothing sufficiently grandiose to attract his highness' approving eye even for a second. It is then that he imagines the axle of the archducal coach, having broken once, breaking again, the coach lurching violently to one side, the carriage door flying open, and the helpless archduchess being hurled out into the snow, where she slides on her many skirts down a relatively gentle slope, not stopping until she, fortunately unhurt, reaches the bottom of the ravine. The mahout's hour has come. With an energetic prod of the stick that sometimes serves as his steering wheel, he directs suleiman to the edge of the ravine and makes him descend slowly and steadily to the place where charles the fifth's daughter lies, still half dazed. Some cuirassiers make as if to follow him, but the archduke stops them, Leave him, let's see how he copes. Barely has he spoken than the archduchess, lifted up by the elephant's trunk, finds herself seated between fritz's spread legs, in a position of physical proximity that, in other circumstances, would seem utterly scandalous. If she were the queen of portugal, she would have to go straight to confession afterwards, that's for sure. Up above, the cuirassiers and the other people in the convoy would be enthusiastically applauding the heroic rescue, while the elephant, apparently aware of what he had done, would climb slowly and steadily back up the slope to the path, where the archduke would embrace his wife and, looking up at the mahout, say in castilian, Muy bien, fritz, gracias. Fritz's soul would have burst right there and then with happiness, always assuming that this were possible in something that is not even pure spirit and if everything we have described were not merely the morbid fruit of a guilty imagination. Reality revealed itself to him exactly as it was, himself hunched on the elephant's back, almost invisible beneath the snow, the desolate image of a defeated conqueror, demonstrating yet again how close the tarpeian rock is to the capitoline hill, on the latter they crown you with laurels and from the former they fling you down, all glory vanished, all honour lost, to the place where you will leave your wretched bones. The axle on the coach did not break again, the archduchess is dozing peacefully, resting her head on her husband's shoulder, unaware that she had been saved by an elephant and that a mahout from portugal had served as an instrument of divine providence. Despite all the criticisms that have been heaped upon the world, it daily discovers ways of functioning tant bien que mal, if you will allow us this small homage to french culture, the proof of which is that when good things don't happen of their own accord in reality, the free imagination helps create a more balanced composition. It's true that the mahout did not save the archduchess, but the fact that he had imagined it meant that he could have done, and that is what counts. He may find himself pitilessly returned to his solitary state and to the icy teeth of the cold and the snow, but thanks to certain fatalistic beliefs internalised or absorbed in lisbon, Fritz considers that if it was written on the tablets of destiny that the archduke would one day make his peace with him, then that day will inevitably arrive. Filled by this comfortable certainty, he abandoned himself to suleiman's rolling gait, once more alone in the landscape, for, in the continuing snow, the rear of the archduke's coach was nowhere in sight. The poor visibility still allowed them to see where they should put their feet, but not where their feet would take them. Meanwhile, the scenery around them had changed, first to something that one might describe as discreet, gentle, almost undulating, now to one so violent it made you think that the mountains must have undergone an apocalyptic series of fractures whose severity had increased in geometric progression. It had taken only twenty leagues to go from rounded spurs that could pass for hills to a tumult of rocks that either split open to form ravines or rose up in peaks that scaled the sky and down whose slopes occasional swift avalanches hurled themselves, thus forming new landscapes and new tracks to delight the skiers of the future. We seem to be approaching the isarco pass, which the austrians insist on calling eisack. We will have to walk for at least another hour before we reach it, but a providential diminution in the thick curtain of snow means that, for a brief moment, we can see it in the distance, a vertical tear in the mountain. The isarco pass, said the mahout. And so it was. It's hard to understand just why the archduke maximilian should have decided to make such a journey at this time of year, but that is how it's set down in history, as an incontrovertible, documented fact, supported by historians and confirmed by the novelist, who must be forgiven for taking certain liberties with names, not only because it is his right to invent, but also because he had to fill in certain gaps so that the sacred coherence of the story was not lost. It must be said that history is always selective, and discriminatory too, selecting from life only what society deems to be historical and scorning the rest, which is precisely where we might find the true explanation of facts, of things, of wretched reality itself. In truth, I say to you, it is better to be a novelist, a fiction writer, a liar. Or a mahout, despite the hare-brained fantasies to which, either by birth or profession, they seem to be prone. Although fritz has no option but to be carried along by suleiman, we have to acknowledge that the edifying story we have been telling would not be the same with another mahout in charge. So far, fritz has been a vital character at every turn, be it dramatic or comic, even at the risk

of cutting a ridiculous figure whenever a pinch of the ludi-
crous was felt to be necessary or merely tactically advisable
for the narrative, putting up with humiliations without a
word of protest or a flicker of emotion, careful not to let it
be known that, without him, there would be no one to deliver
the goods, or in this case, to take the elephant to vienna.
These remarks may seem unnecessary to readers more interested in the dynamic of the text than in general expressions
of supposed solidarity, but it was clear that fritz, after recent
disastrous events, needed someone to place a friendly hand
on his shoulder, and that is all we did, place a hand on his
shoulder. When the mind wanders, when it carries us off on
the wings of daydreams, we do not even notice the distances
travelled, especially when the feet carrying us are not our
own. Apart from the odd stray flake that has lost its way, it
has pretty much stopped snowing now. The narrow path
ahead of us is the famous isarco pass. Rising almost verti-
cally on either side, the walls of the ravine seem about to
crash down onto the path. Fritz's heart contracted with fear,
his bones were filled with a cold quite different from anything
he had ever known before. He was alone in the midst of that
terrible all-pervading threat, for the archduke's imperative
orders that the convoy should remain united and cohesive
as their sole guarantee of safety, just as mountaineers rope
themselves together, had been quite simply ignored. A
proverb, if it can be called such, and which is as portuguese
as it is indian and universal, sums up such situations elegantly
and eloquently, do as I tell you, not as I do. That is precisely
how the archduke had behaved, he had given an order, Stay
together, but when it came to it, instead of waiting, as he
should have done, for the elephant and his mahout who
were following behind, especially given that he was the owner

of one and the master of the other, he had, figuratively speaking, dug his spurs into his horse and legged it, straight for the far end of the dangerous pass before it was too late and darkness fell. But just imagine if the vanguard of cuirassiers had ridden into the pass and waited there for those behind them to catch up, the archduke and his arch-duchess, the elephant suleiman and the mahout fritz, the cart carrying the forage, and finally their fellow cuirassiers bringing up the rear, as well as all the wagons in between, laden with coffers and chests and trunks, and the multitude of servants, all fraternally gathered, waiting for the mountain to fall on them or for such an avalanche as had never before been seen to shroud them all in snow, blocking the pass until springtime. Egotism, generally held to be one of the most negative and repudiated of human characteristics, can, in certain circumstances, have its good side. Having saved our own precious skin, by fleeing the deadly mouse-trap that the isarco pass had become, we also saved the skins of our travelling companions, who, when they arrived, could continue on their way unobstructed by untimely bottlenecks of traffic, the conclusion, therefore, is easy to draw, every man for himself so that all can be saved. Who would have thought it, not only is a moral act not always what it appears to be, but the more it contradicts itself the more effective it is. Faced by such crystal-clear proofs and roused by the sudden thud, a hundred yards behind them, of a mass of snow, which, while not aspiring to the name of avalanche, was more than enough to give them a real fright, fritz signalled to suleiman to get walking, now. This order seemed to suleiman rather on the conservative side. Such a perilous situation called not for a walk, but a trot or, better still, a rapid gallop that would save him from the dangers of the isarco pass. Rapid it was, as rapid as saint anthony when he used the fourth dimension to travel to lisbon and save his father from the gallows. Unfortunately, suleiman overestimated his own strength. A few metres after he had left the pass behind him, his front legs crumpled under him and he knelt down, lungs bursting. The mahout, however, was lucky. Such a fall would normally have sent him flying over the head of his unfortunate mount, with god alone knows what tragic consequences, but in suleiman's celebrated elephantine memory there surfaced the recollection of what had happened with the village priest who tried to exorcise him, when, at the last second, at the very last moment, he, suleiman, had softened the blow he had unleashed and that would otherwise have proved fatal. The difference now was that suleiman somehow managed to use what little reserves of energy he had left to reduce the impetus of his own fall, so that his huge knees touched the ground as lightly as a snowflake. How he did this, we have no idea, and we're not going to ask him either. Like magicians, elephants have their secrets. When forced to choose between speaking and remaining silent, an elephant always chooses silence, that is why his trunk grew so long, so that, apart from being capable of transporting tree trunks and serving as an elevator for his mahout, it has the added advantage of being a serious obstacle to any bouts of uncontrolled loquacity. Fritz carefully intimated to suleiman that it was time to make a small effort and get to his feet. He didn't order him, he didn't resort to any of his varied repertoire of flicks and pokes with the stick, some more aggressive than others, he merely intimated his wishes to him, which shows yet again that respect for other people's feelings is the best way to ensure a prosperous and happy life as regards one's relationships and affections. It's the difference between a categorical Get up and a tentative What about trying to get up. There are even those who maintain that jesus actually used the latter phrase and not the former, which provides absolute proof that the resurrection was, ultimately, dependent on lazarus' free will and not on the nazarene's miraculous powers, however sublime they may have been. If lazarus came back to life it was because he was spoken to kindly, as simple as that. And it was clear that the method continues to produce good results, for suleiman, straightening first his right leg and then his left, restored fritz to the relative safety of a rather uncertain verticality, since, up until then, fritz had been entirely dependent on a few stiff hairs on the back of the elephant's neck if he was not to be precipitated down suleiman's trunk. Suleiman is now back on his four feet, suddenly cheered by the arrival of the forage cart which, having battled through the aforementioned mound of snow, thanks to valiant work from the two yoke of oxen, was moving at a sprightly pace towards the end of the pass and the elephant's voracious appetite. Suleiman's almost failing soul now received its reward for the remarkable feat of having restored life to its own prostrate body, which, in the middle of that cruel, white landscape, had looked as if it would never rise again. The table was set right there and then, and while fritz and the ox-driver were celebrating their salvation with a few swigs of brandy provided by the latter, suleiman was devouring bundle after bundle of forage with touching enthusiasm. All that was lacking was for flowers to bloom in the snow and for the little birds of spring to return to the tyrol and sing their sweet songs. But you can't have everything. It's quite enough that fritz and the ox-driver, putting their two intelligences together, should have found a solution to a worrying tendency among the various components of the convoy to drift apart as if they had nothing to do with each other. It was, shall we say, a bipartite solution, but doubtless a precursor to a different way of approaching problems, that is, even if the aim of the scheme is to serve one's own interests, it's always a good idea to know that one can count on the other party. An integrated solution, in other words. From now on, the oxen and the elephant will, at all times, travel together, the forage cart in front and the elephant behind, with the smell of the hay in his nostrils, so to speak. However logical and rational the topographical distribution of this small group may appear, and as no one would dare to deny, nothing of what has been achieved here, thanks to a genuine desire for unanimity, will apply, well, how could it, to the archduke and archduchess, whose coach has gone on ahead, indeed, it may even have reached bressanone already. If that is so, we are authorised to reveal that suleiman will enjoy a richly deserved two weeks of rest in this well-known tourist spot, in an inn called am hohen feld, which means, appropriately enough, steep land. It's only natural that it will strike some as strange that an inn located in italian territory should have a german name, but this is easily explained when we remember that most of the guests who come here are austrians and germans who like to feel at home. For similar reasons, in the algarve, as someone will later take the trouble to point out, a praia will no longer be called a praia but a beach, a pescador a fisherman, whether he likes it or not, and, as for tourist complexes, they will no longer be called aldeias, but holiday villages, villages de vacances or ferienorte. Things will reach such a pitch that there will no longer be any lojas de modas, because these will be called, in a kind of portuguese by adoption, a boutique and, in english, inevitably, fashion shop, less inevitably, modes in french, and quite bluntly modegeschäft in german. A sapataria will become a shoe shop, and that will be that. And if a traveller were to start collecting the names of bars and nightclubs, like someone hunting for lice, by the time he had gone all around the coast to sines, he would still know hardly a word of portuguese. So despised is that language there that one could say of the algarve, in an age when the civilised are descending into barbarism, that it is the land of portuguese as she is not spoke. And bressanone is the same.

It is said, once tolstoy had said it first, that all happy families are alike, and there is really little more to say about them. It would seem that the same is true of happy elephants. One need look no further than suleiman. During the two weeks he spent in bressanone, he rested, slept, ate and drank his fill, until he could eat no more, demolishing something like four tons of forage and drinking about three thousand litres of water, thus making up for the many enforced slimming regimes imposed on him during his long journey through the lands of portugal, spain and italy, when it wasn't always possible to replenish his larder on a regular basis. Now that suleiman has recovered his strength, he is plump and handsome, after only a week, his flaccid, wrinkled skin has ceased to hang in folds about him like a coat on a hook. The archduke was given the good news and made a point of visiting the elephant in his house, or, rather, stable, rather than having him parade around in the square simply to show off suleiman's now excellent physical form and magnificent appearance to himself, the archduchess and the assembled populace. Naturally, fritz was present at this visit, but, conscious that the reconciliation between him and the archduke had not been formalised, if indeed it ever would be, he was discreet and solicitous, careful not to draw attention to himself, but hopeful that the archduke would, at the very least, utter some brief words of congratulation or praise. And so it was. At the end of the visit, the archduke shot him a rapid glance and said, You've done a good job, fritz, suleiman must be very pleased, to which fritz replied, That is all I desire, sir, my life is at your highness's service. The archduke did not respond, apart from muttering a laconic Hmm, a primitive sound, if not the very first, and one which every man is at liberty to interpret as he wishes. Fritz was predisposed by temperament and philosophy of life to take an optimistic view of events, and despite the apparent brusqueness of that grunt and the inappropriateness of such a sound in the mouth of an arch-duke and soon-to-be emperor, fritz interpreted it as a step, a small, but definite step, in the direction of much-desired concord. Let us wait until vienna to see what happens.

The distance from bressanone to the brenner pass is so short that there surely won't be time for the convoy to become dispersed. Neither time nor distance. Which means that we will bump up against the same moral dilemma we met before in the isarco pass, namely, should we travel together or separately. It's frightening just to imagine the whole long convoy, from the cuirassiers in the vanguard to those bringing up the rear, being stuck between the walls of the ravine and under constant threat from avalanches or rockfalls. It's probably best to leave the solution of this problem in god's hands and let him decide. Just keep moving and see what happens. This anxiety, however understand-able, should not make us forget another worrying factor. According to people who know, the brenner pass is ten times more dangerous than the isarco pass, others say twenty times, adding that every year it claims a few victims, buried beneath avalanches or crushed by the huge boulders that roll down the mountainside, even though, when their fall begins, there is nothing about them that indicates such a fateful destiny. Let's hope that a time will come when, by building viaducts that span the heights, they can do away with these deep passes in which we are already almost buried alive. The inter-esting thing is that the people obliged to travel through these passes always do so with a kind of fatalistic resignation, which, while it may not prevent their bodies from being assailed by fear, at least appears to leave their souls intact and serene, like a steadily burning light that no hurricane could extinguish. People say a lot of things, and not all of them are true, but that is what human beings are like, they can as easily believe that the hair of an elephant, marinated in a little oil, can cure baldness, as imagine that they carry within them the one solitary light that will lead them along life's paths, even through mountain passes. One way or another, as the wise old hermit of the alps once said, we will all have to die.

The weather is not good, which, at this time of year, as has been abundantly demonstrated, is hardly a novelty. It's true that the snow is falling only lightly and that visibility is almost normal, but the wind's chill blasts are like sharp blades come to cut through our clothes, however warm. Just ask the cuirassiers. According to the rumour doing the rounds, the reason they are setting out today is because the meteorological situation is expected to worsen tomorrow, and because, once we have travelled a few kilometres further north, the worst of the alps will, in theory, be behind us. In other words, strike before you are struck. Many of bressanone's inhabitants came to watch the departure of the archduke maximilian and his elephant and were rewarded with a surprise. When the archduke and his wife were about to enter their carriage, suleiman knelt down on the frozen ground, a gesture that provoked a flurry of applause and cheers loud enough to merit being set down in the records. The archduke began to smile, but his smile immediately turned to a frown at the thought that this new miracle was probably a crafty manœuvre on the part of fritz, desperate to make peace with him. The noble archduke is quite wrong, the elephant's gesture was entirely spontaneous and sprang, if we may put it so, from his soul, it was a way of saying thank you to those who most deserved his thanks, for the excellent treatment meted out to him at the am hohen feld inn during the two weeks he spent there, a whole fortnight of perfect happiness and, therefore, happily uneventful. Although one should also not exclude the possibility that our elephant, quite rightly concerned by the obvious cooling in relations between his mahout and the archduke, intended this charming gesture as a way of pouring oil on troubled waters, as people will say in the future and then cease to say. Then again, so that we are not accused of partiality by perhaps ignoring the real key to the matter, we cannot exclude the hypothesis, not merely academic, that fritz, either deliberately or accidentally, touched suleiman's right ear with his stick, and as we saw from what happened in padua, that ear was a miracle-working organ par excellence. We should know by now that the most exact, most precise representation of the human heart is the labyrinth. And where the human heart is involved, anything is possible.

The convoy is ready to depart. There is a general feeling of apprehension and overt anxiety, it is clear that people cannot get out of their minds the idea of the brenner pass and all its dangers. And the chronicler of these events has no qualms in confessing that he fears he may lack the ability to describe the famous pass that lies ahead, an inability he had to disguise as best he could at the isarco pass by diverting the reader onto secondary matters, which, while possibly of importance in themselves, were clearly a way of sidestepping the fundamental issue. It's a shame that photography had not yet been invented in the sixteenth century, because then the solution would have been as easy as pie, we would simply have included a few photos from the period, especially if taken from a helicopter, and readers would then have every reason to consider themselves amply rewarded and to recognise the extraordinarily informative nature of our enterprise. By the way, it is time we mentioned that the next small town, a very short distance from bressanone, is called in italian, given that we're still in italy, vitipeno. The fact that the austrians and germans call it sterzing is beyond our comprehension. Nevertheless, we would accept the possibility, although we'd stop short of actually putting our hand in the fire, that italian is still more widely spoken here than portuguese is in the algarve.

We have left bressanone now. It's hard to understand why in such a rugged region as this, where there is no shortage of vertiginous mountain ranges one after the other, it was thought necessary to gouge out such deep scars as the isarco and the brenner pass, rather than putting them in places on the planet less blessed with natural beauty, where such exceptional, amazing geological phenomena could, with the aid of the tourist industry, materially benefit the modest, long-suffering lives of the local inhabitants. Contrary to what you might, quite rightly, think, bearing in mind our problems when it came to describing the isarco pass, these comments are not intended to replace the foreseeable paucity of descriptions of the brenner pass that we are about to enter. They are merely a humble recognition of how much truth is contained in that well-known phrase, Words fail me. Because words really do fail us. They say that in one of the languages spoken by the indigenous peoples of south america, possibly in amazonia, there are more than twenty ways, about twenty-seven we seem to recall, of describing the colour green.

Compared with the poverty of our own vocabulary in that respect, you would think it would be easy for them to describe the forests in which they live, in the midst of all those minutely differentiated greens, distinguished by subtle, almost imperceptible nuances. We don't know that they ever tried nor, if they did, whether they were satisfied with the result. What we do know is that a monochromatic approach won't solve the problem, why, one need look no further than the apparently pure whiteness of these mountains, because, for all we know, there may be more than twenty different shades of white that the eye cannot perceive, but whose existence it can intuit. The truth, if we want to accept it in all its crudity, is that it's simply not possible to describe a landscape in words. Or rather, it's possible, but not worthwhile. I wonder if it's even worth writing the word mountain when we don't know what name the mountain would give itself. Painting, though, is a different matter, it's perfectly capable of creating on the palette twenty-seven different shades of green that have eluded nature, plus a few others that don't even seem green, but that, of course, is what we call art. Painted trees do not lose their leaves.

We are now inside the brenner pass. On the archduke's express orders, utter silence reigns. This time, the convoy, as if fear had produced a congregational effect, shows not the slightest tendency to disperse, the muzzles of the horses drawing the archduke's carriage are almost touching the hindquarters of the cuirassiers' horses immediately in front, suleiman is so close to the archduchess's little bottle of perfume that he can breathe in the delicious scent that issues from it whenever the daughter of charles the fifth feels a need to refresh herself. The rest of the convoy, beginning with the ox-cart carrying the forage and the water trough, follows right behind as if there were no other way to reach their destination. Everyone is shivering with cold, but also, and above all, with fear. The tortuous crevices of the sheer escarpments are filled with the snow that occasionally breaks free and falls with a dull thud on the convoy, and these small avalanches, while not dangerous in themselves, only serve to increase the levels of fear. No one feels confident enough to use their eyes to enjoy the beauty of the landscape, although there are those familiar with the place who remark to their neighbour, It's much prettier here when there's no snow, What do you mean prettier, asked their companion, intrigued, Well, it's not really something you can put into words. The greatest disrespect we can show for reality, whatever that reality might be, when attempting the pointless task of describing a landscape, is to do so with words that are not our own and never were, by which we mean words that have already appeared on millions of pages and in millions of mouths before our turn to use them finally comes, weary words, exhausted from being passed from hand to hand, leaving in each one part of their vital substance. If we were to write, for example, the words crystalline stream, so often used in describing landscapes, we never stop to wonder if the stream is still as crystalline as it was when we saw it for the first time, or if it has ceased to be a stream and become instead a rushing river, or, unhappy fate, the foulest and most malodorous of swamps. It may not seem so at first sight, but all of this is closely related to our earlier brave affirmation that it is simply not possible to describe a landscape or, by extension, anything else. In the mouth of a trusted person who, for example, knows these places as they appear at all the different seasons of the year, such words would give us food for thought. If that person, in all honesty and basing himself on long experience, were to say that it's impossible to describe what your eyes see by translating it into words, whether it be snow or a garden in full bloom, how could anyone dare to do so who has never in his life been through the brenner pass and certainly not in the sixteenth century, when there were no motorways or petrol stations, hot snacks and cups of coffee, not to mention a motel where you could spend the night in the warm, while outside the storm rages and a lost elephant utters the most anguished of cries. We were not there, we have been guided by whatever information we could garner, possibly of dubious value, for example, an old engraving, deserving of our respect only because of its great age and ingenuous design, shows an elephant in hannibal's army falling into a ravine when, according to the experts, during the carthaginian army's laborious crossing of the alps, not one elephant was lost. No one was lost here either. The convoy is still keeping together, close and resolute, qualities that are no less praiseworthy for being based, as we explained earlier, on entirely selfish motives. There are, however, exceptions. The cuirassiers' biggest concern, for example, has nothing to do with their own personal safety, but with that of their horses, obliged now to walk on slippery, compacted, blue-grey ice, where a metacarpal fracture would have the most fatal of consequences. However this may rankle with the stubborn lutheranism of archduke maximilian the second of austria, the miracle performed by suleiman at the door of the basilica of saint anthony in padua has so far protected the convoy, not only the powerful people travelling in it, but the ordinary ones too, which stands as proof, if proof were needed, of the rare and excellent thaumaturgical virtues of a saint who was born fernando de bulhões and over whom two cities, lisbon and padua, have been arguing for centuries, rather pointlessly it must be said, because it is clear to everyone that padua ended up flying the flag of victory, while lisbon had to make do with parades through the streets, red wine, grilled sardines, as well as balloons and pots of marjoram. It isn't enough to know how and where fernando de bulhões was born, one has to wait and find out how and where saint anthony will die.

It's still snowing and, if you'll forgive the slight vulgarity of the expression, it's absolutely perishing. Immense care must be taken when walking because of the wretched ice, but, although we have not yet seen the back of the mountains, our lungs seem to breathe more easily, seem less constricted, free now from the strangely oppressive feeling that descends from the inaccessible heights. The next town is innsbruck, on the banks of the river inn, and, unless the archduke has abandoned the idea he mentioned to his steward while they were still in bressanone, much of the distance that separates us from vienna is to be covered by boat, downstream, first on the river inn as far as passau, and then on the danube, mighty rivers both, especially the danube, which, in austria, is called the donau. It is more than likely that we will have a quiet journey, as quiet as our two-week stay in bressanone, during which nothing of note happened, no burlesque episode to be recounted of an evening, no ghost story to tell the grandchildren, and that is why people felt particularly fortunate, having arrived safe and sound at the am hohen feld inn, far from their families, all anxieties postponed, any creditors forced to rein in their impatience, no compromising letter fallen into the wrong hands, in short, the future, as the ancients used to say, belongs to god alone, so seize the day and trust not in the morrow. This change to the itinerary is not merely some whim of the archduke's, although it does now include two visits that were partly courtesy calls and partly to do with lofty matters concerning the political situation in central europe, the first to the duke of bavaria in wasserburg, the second, rather longer, to müldhorf, to see ernst, also duke of bavaria, prince-archbishop of salzburg. But returning to the subject of roads, it is true that the road from innsbruck to vienna is relatively good, with no cataclysmic geological features like the alps, and although it may not follow a completely straight line, it is at least pretty sure of where it's going. However, the advantage of rivers is that they are like roads that can walk, they can travel under their own steam, especially such mighty rivers as the inn and the danube. The greatest beneficiary of this change will be suleiman who, if he needs a drink, will have only to go over to the side of the boat, stick his trunk in the water and suck. On the other hand, he would not be at all pleased if he knew what a chronicler from the riverside town of hall just outside innsbruck, a scribe called franz schweyher, had written, Maximilian returned in splendour from spain, bringing with him an elephant that is twelve feet tall and mouse-coloured. Given what we know of Suleiman, his riposte would have been quick, direct and incisive, It isn't elephants who are mouse-coloured, it's mice who are elephant-coloured. And he would add, A little more respect, please.

Swaying to the rhythm of suleiman's stately step, fritz brushes off the snow that has adhered to his eyebrows and wonders what his future in vienna will be, he's a mahout and will continue to be a mahout, nor could he ever be anything else, but the memory of his time in lisbon, where he was initially feted by the populace, even nobles from the royal court, who are, strictly speaking, also members of the populace, then promptly forgotten by everyone, leads him to ask himself if, in vienna, they will also place him in a stockade with the elephant and leave him there to rot. Something is sure to happen, solomon, he said, this journey has been only an interval, and just be glad that the mahout subhro has given you back your real name, you will have the life, be it good or bad, for which you were born and from which you cannot escape, but I wasn't born to be a mahout, in fact, no man was born to be a mahout even if no other door opens for him in his entire existence, basically, I'm a kind of parasite on you, a louse hidden among the bristles on your back, I probably won't live for as long as you will, men's lives are short compared with those of elephants, that's a known fact, I wonder what will become of you if I'm not around, they'll summon another mahout, of course, someone will have to take care of suleiman, perhaps the archduchess will offer her services, that would be funny, an archduchess serving an elephant, or else one of the princes when they're grown up, but, one way or another, dear friend, while your future is guaranteed, mine isn't, I'm a mahout, a parasite, a mere appendage.

Weary from such a long journey, we reached innsbruck on a notable date in the catholic calendar, epiphany, in the year fifteen hundred and fifty-two. There was a terrific party as one would expect in the first big austrian town to welcome the archduke. It's not quite clear whether the applause was for him or for the elephant, not that this matters much to the future emperor, for whom suleiman is, apart from anything else, a political tool of the first order, whose importance could never be diminished by petty jealousy. The success of their reception in wasserburg and müldhorf is bound to owe something to the presence of a creature hitherto unknown in austria, as if maximilian the second had conjured it out of thin air to please his subjects, from the lowest to the highest. The whole final stage of the elephant's journey will be a constant joyful clamour that will spread from one town to another like wildfire, as well as providing inspiration to the artists and poets of each place we pass through and who will outdo themselves producing paintings, engravings and commemorative medals, or composing poetic inscriptions like those written by the well-known humanist caspar bruschius, intended for the town hall of linz. And speaking of linz, where the convoy will abandon ships, boats and rafts to continue the rest of the journey on foot, it is only natural that someone will want to know why the archduke didn't continue on in comfort down the river, since the same river danube that brought them to linz would also have taken them on to vienna. Such thoughts are at best naïve and, at worst, ignorant, showing, as they do, a complete failure to grasp the importance in the lives of nations in general and of politics and other commercial enterprises in particular of a well-thought-out publicity campaign. What would happen if archduke maximilian of austria were to make the mistake of disembarking in the port of vienna. Now, ports, whether large or small, whether they serve river or sea, have never been noted for their orderliness or cleanliness, and when, by chance, they present themselves to us with every appearance of organised normality, it is wise to remember that such an appearance is merely one of the countless and not infrequently contradictory faces of chaos. What would happen if the archduke were to disembark along with all his convoy, elephant included, onto a quay crammed with crates and sacks and sundry bundles, in the midst of all that detritus, with the crowds getting in the way, just how would he manage to make his way through to the city's new avenues and there prepare for a proper parade. It would be a very sad entrance after more than three years' absence. And that is not what will happen. In müldhorf, the archduke will give orders to his steward to draw up plans for a reception party in vienna befitting the event, or events, firstly, and most obviously, the arrival of himself and the archduchess, secondly, the arrival of that marvel of nature, the elephant suleiman, who will astonish the viennese just as he has astonished all those who laid eyes on him in portugal, spain and italy, which, to be fair, are not exactly barbarous lands. Messengers on horseback left for vienna with orders intended for the burgermeister, orders in which the archduke expressed his wish to see reflected in people's hearts and in the streets all the love that he and the archduchess felt for the city. Well, a nod is as good as a wink to a blind man. Other instructions were issued, for internal use only, suggesting that it would be a good idea to take advantage of the journey down the rivers inn and danube to carry out a general clean-up of people and animals, although, since, for understandable reasons, this could not include bathing in the ice-cold waters of the river, said clean-up would have to be a fairly superficial affair. Every morning, the archduke and archduchess were provided with a goodly quantity of hot water for their ablutions, and this led those members of the convoy concerned with their own personal hygiene to sigh sadly and murmur, I wish I was an archduke. They didn't want the power that maximilian the second held in his hands, indeed, they might not even have known what to do with it, but they did covet that hot water, about whose utility they appeared to have no doubts.

When he disembarked in linz, the archduke already had very clear ideas about how to organise the convoy to his best advantage, especially as regards the psychological impact of his return on the population of vienna, which was, after all, the capital and, therefore, a place of heightened political sensibilities. The cuirassiers, who had up until then been divided into vanguard and rearguard, became one unit at the head of the convoy. Immediately behind them came the elephant, which, we must admit, was a strategic move worthy of an alekhine, especially when we learn that the archduke's carriage will come only third in the convoy. The objective was clear, to give greatest prominence to suleiman, which made perfect sense, since vienna had seen archdukes of austria before, whereas this would be their first sighting of an elephant. It is thirty-two leagues from linz to vienna and there will be two planned intermediate stops, one in melk and the other in the town of amstetten, where they will sleep, small stages, so that the convoy can enter vienna looking reasonably fresh. The weather is far from perfect, the snow continues to fall and the wind has still not lost its cutting edge, but compared with the isarco and brenner passes, this could easily be the road to paradise, although it's unlikely that roads exist in that celestial place, because souls, once they've fulfilled the necessary entrance requirements, are immediately equipped with a pair of wings, the only authorised means of locomotion up there. There will be no further rest after amstetten. The people from the villages came down to the road to see the archduke and found themselves face to face with an animal of whom they had vaguely heard and who provoked both understandable curiosity and the most absurd explanations, as happened to the lad who, when he asked his grandfather why the elephant was called an elephant, received the answer, Because he has a trunk. An austrian, even one from the lower classes, is not just anyone, he always has to know everything. Another idea that sprang up among these good people, as we tend so patronisingly to call them, was that in suleiman's country of origin everyone owned an elephant, just as here people owned a horse, a mule, or more often a donkey, and that they must be pretty rich if they could afford to feed an animal that size. The proof of this came when we had to stop in the middle of the road so that suleiman could eat, because for some unknown reason, he had turned up his nose at break-fast. A small crowd gathered round, amazed at the speed with which the elephant, with the aid of his trunk, stuffed the bundles of hay into his mouth and swallowed them, having first turned them over a couple of times with his powerful molars, which, although invisible from the outside, were easy enough to imagine. As the convoy neared vienna, there was a gradual but noticeable improvement in the weather. Nothing extraordinary, there was still a lot of low cloud, but it had stopped snowing. Someone said, If it goes on like this, we'll arrive in vienna with a clear blue sky and in brilliant sunshine. That isn't quite what happened, but things would have been very different on this journey if the weather in general had followed the example of what will one day become known as the city of the waltz. Now and then, the convoy was obliged to stop because the men and women from the surrounding villages wanted to show off their singing and dancing skills, which particu-larly pleased the archduchess, whose pleasure the archduke shared in a benevolent, almost fatherly manner, corres-ponding to a still common attitude, What do you expect, that's women for you. The towers and domes of vienna were already on the horizon, the doors of the city stood wide open, and the people were out in the streets and in the squares, dressed in their best clothes in honour of the archduke and archduchess. That is how valladolid had greeted the elephant too, but iberian folk are as easily pleased as children. Here, in austrian vienna, they cultivate discipline and order, there's something almost teutonic about it, as the future will show. The most powerful figure of authority is arriving in the city, and what prevails among the population is a feeling of respect and unconditional deference. Life, however, has many cards up its sleeve and often produces them when we least expect it. The elephant was proceeding unhurriedly, at a measured pace, the pace of one who knows that more haste does not necessarily mean more speed. Suddenly, a girl of about five, as we later learned, who was watching the cortège with her parents, let go of her mother's hand and ran towards the elephant. A horrified gasp left the throats of all those who could foresee the tragedy about to unfold, the animal's feet knocking down and trampling the poor little body, the archduke's return besmirched by misfortune, national mourning, the terrible blot on the city's escutcheon. They clearly did not know solomon. He coiled his trunk around the girl's body as if in an embrace and lifted her into the air like a new flag, the flag of a life saved at the very last moment, when it was about to be lost. The girl's weeping parents ran to solomon and received in their arms their daughter, restored, brought back to life, while everyone else applauded, many of them dissolving into tears of uncontrolled emotion, some saying that it had been a miracle, quite unaware of the miracle solomon had performed in padua by kneeling at the door

of the basilica of saint anthony. And then, as if the denoue-
ment of the dramatic incident we have just witnessed were
not quite complete, the archduke was seen to step down
from his carriage before helping the archduchess down as
well, whereupon both of them, hand in hand, walked over
to the elephant, who was still surrounded by people cheering
him as the hero of the day, and as he would continue to be
for a long time afterwards, for the story of the elephant who
saved a little viennese girl from certain death will be told a
thousand times and elaborated upon a thousand times more,
even now. When the people realised that the archduke and
archduchess were approaching, silence fell, and the crowd
made way for them. Shock was still evident on many faces,
some of the onlookers were even having difficulty drying
their tears. Fritz had descended from the elephant's back
and was waiting. The archduke stopped and looked him
straight in the eye. Fritz bowed his head and saw before
him the archduke's right hand, open and expectant, Sir, I
do not dare, he said, and held out his own hands, dirty
from continuous contact with the elephant's skin, who was,
nevertheless, still the cleaner of the two, since fritz could
not remember when he'd last had a proper bath, whereas
suleiman cannot pass a pool of water without plunging into
it. When the archduke still did not withdraw his hand, fritz
had no alternative but to shake it, his hard, calloused
mahout's skin touching the fine, delicate skin of a man who
had never even had to dress himself. Then the archduke
said, Thank you for avoiding a tragedy, But I didn't do
anything, sir, suleiman deserves all the praise, That may be
so, but you, I imagine, must have contributed in some way,
Well, I did what I could, sir, I wouldn't be a mahout otherwise, If everyone did what they could, the world would

doubtless be a better place, If your highness says so, it must be true, You're forgiven, there's no need for flattery, Thank you, sir, Welcome to vienna and I hope vienna deserves both you and suleiman, you'll be happy here. And with that, maximilian went back to his carriage, leading the archduchess by the hand. Charles the fifth's daughter is pregnant yet again.

The elephant died less than two years later, when it was once more winter, in the final month of fifteen hundred and fifty three. The cause of death was never known, at the time there were no blood tests, chest x-rays, endoscopies, mri scans or any of the other things that are now everyday occurrences for humans, although less so for animals, who die with no nurse to place a hand upon their fevered brow. As well as skinning solomon, they cut off his front legs so that, once duly cleaned and cured, they could serve as recipients, at the entrance to the palace, for walking sticks, canes, umbrellas and sunshades in summer. As you see, kneeling before the archduke did solomon no good at all. The mahout subhro received from the hands of the steward the part of his salary that was owing to him, to which was added, by order of the archduke, a rather generous tip, and with that money, he bought a mule on which to ride and a donkey to carry the box containing his few possessions. He announced that he was going back to lisbon, but there is no record of him having entered the country. He must either have changed his mind or died en route.

Weeks later, the archduke's letter reached the portuguese court. In it, he informed them that the elephant suleiman had died, but that the inhabitants of vienna would never forget him, for he had saved the life of a child on the very day he arrived in the city. The first reader of the letter was the secretary of state, pêro de alcáçova carneiro, who handed it to the king, saying, Solomon has died, sir. Dom joão the third looked surprised at first and then a shadow of grief darkened his face. Summon the queen, he said. Dona catarina was quick to arrive, as if she sensed that the letter brought news of interest to her, perhaps a birth or a wedding. It was clearly neither a birth nor a wedding, for her husband's face told quite another story. Dom joão the third said softly, Our cousin maximilian writes to say that solomon. The queen would not allow him to finish, I don't want to know, she cried, I don't want to know. And she ran off and shut herself in her room, where she wept for the rest of the day.

Translator's acknowledgements

I would like to thank Tânia Ganho, Ben Sherriff and Euan Cameron for all their help and advice.

penguin.co.uk/vintage